Perfect
FOR
FRAMING

Other books by
MAGGIE BISHOP

The Appalachian Adventure Series
Appalachian Paradise
Emeralds in the Snow
Murder at Blue Falls

Perfect FOR FRAMING

by

Maggie Bishop

High Country Publishers

INGALLS PUBLISHING GROUP, INC
Boone, NC
2008

High Country Publishers
INGALLS PUBLISHING GROUP, INC.
197 New Market Center #135
Boone, NC 28607

www.ingallspublishinggroup.com

Copyright © 2008 by Maggie Bishop

This is a work of fiction. All characters, places and events are products of the author's imagination or are used fictitiously. Any resemblance to persons living or dead is purely coincidental.

Book design by Ann Thompson Nemcosky

Library of Congress Cataloging-in-Publication Data
Bishop, Maggie, 1949-
    Perfect for framing / by Maggie Bishop.
         p. cm. -- (An Appalachian adventure mystery)
    ISBN 978-1-932158-84-7 (trade pbk. : alk. paper)
1. Woodwork--Fiction.
2. Appalachian Region, Southern--Fiction. 3. North Carolina--Fiction. I. Title.
    PS3602.I76P47 2008
    813'.6--dc22
         2008027837

First Printing, November 2008

Acknowledgments

Husband Bob Gillman for love and patience

Parents Pearle & Lyle Bishop for love and my first computer

Judith Geary, editor & author of *Getorix*

Barbara & Bob Ingalls, publishers, for believing in my stories

Dee Dee Rominger, Captain of Investigations, Watauga County Sheriff's department

John Rainey of Saslow's Jeweler's for allowing me to photograph bracelet & use of name

Jane Wilson, author, for use of her recipes

Ree Strawser for photography information

Norma Green and Lisa Haynes of the Ford Dealership in Boone, NC

Nora Percival, author of *Weather of the Heart*, for critiquing

Clinton Triplett for use of himself and his alter ego, Elvis

Cast of Characters

Jemma Chase – *carpenter, trail ride leader, photographer, CSI wannabe*

Alma Chase – *Blue Falls Ranch cook and temporary director, Jemma's aunt.*

Detective Tucker – *Watauga County Sheriff's Department detective*

Detective Graves – *Detective Tucker's partner*

Ann Dixon – *Perfect for Framing gallery owner*

Karen Harmon – *Jemma's customer in Hickory Hills subdivision, friend of Ann Dixon*

Darryl Johnson – *Star Lite Properties owner*

Flora Johnson – *wife of real estate owner, friend of Ann Dixon*

Randy Kincaid – *Blue Falls Ranch neighbor and beau of Alma Chase*

Lottie Miller – *widow of carpenter, great grandmother of Travis*

Travis Miller – *mechanic at Ford dealership*

Petula Windsor – *Properties Owners Association President, part-time receptionist at Star Lite Prop*

Ward Windsor – *husband of Petula Windsor, banker*

Raymond Viccaro – *Ford salesman, stepbrother of Petula*

Perfect
FOR
FRAMING

by

Maggie Bishop

PROLOGUE

PETULA ROSE FROM HER lover's bed, paraded naked to the vanity mirror, and finger combed her hair so it fell over one eye.

"Your bruises are almost gone," the man said.

She smiled at him then studied herself in the mirror. "The lipo doctor did a thorough job. He took six pounds and three inches off my mid-section. I wish these numb spots would go away."

"Give it time, Pet. Your face is almost healed." He propped himself up with her pillow and reached for his cigarettes.

"I hope I'll look better than this soon," Pet said, still studying herself in the mirror. "I thought you gave up those things."

"After this one. I'm down to a couple a day. Besides, you said the same thing after your face lift – no more plastic surgery."

"A lady has a right to change her mind," she called as she stepped into the shower.

By the time she was dressed and had put on makeup, he had his jeans back on. "I'm still mad you let someone buy that lot I wanted to build on," he said as she emerged from the dressing area in her guest house. He pulled on a crumpled polo shirt.

"Don't you worry. I'm in the perfect position to make their lives miserable. Didn't I make it too tough for the last owners to build? I wasn't President of the POA a couple of years ago when you wanted to put your modular on that lot. Now I have the other homeowners in my grip. If you can't build there, no one can."

He dropped the butt into the beer can and hugged her, resting his chin on her head. He said, "Revenge can be so sweet. Maybe you can bankrupt the POA with a lawsuit." He let her go and sat down to tie his sneakers. then asked, "What are you doing with that situation with your husband? Any progress?"

"Don't you worry about that either. I'll end up with the house and a big alimony settlement. Then it'll be just the two of us."

Chapter 1
DECEMBER, THURSDAY

"*T*HAT'S OUTRAGEOUS EVEN for Madam President," Karen said into the phone. "She's going to get herself killed one of these days. Come to think of it, that might be a relief to a lot of us."

At the mention of a murder, Jemma's measuring tape clattered to the floor as she stared at her customer. Jemma Chase wasn't eavesdropping, exactly.

"She must be getting a kick out of playing god again, lording over your land, teasing you with delays. The power-hungry little demon. Murder by hanging would be too easy for her." Karen Harmon grinned into the telephone. After a moment she laughed, then said, "Maybe she could be in a horrible car accident, complete with head through the windshield, destroying the doctor's latest work. Would serve her right for using a Florida plastic surgeon who gave her that uneven hair line." Karen glanced at Jemma who quickly closed her mouth. Karen winked before continuing her phone conversation. "She deserves a spike through her heart, if she had one. She has the sculpted look of a cemetery angel and the attitude of a pit bull. There's not enough Botox and filler in the world to plump up her shrunken heart."

Karen snapped her gum as she hung up the phone. "Our illustrious POA President is at it again," she said to Jemma. "Honey, give a petty person a little power and they'll abuse it every time."

Jemma nodded and retrieved the tape measure, her dream of playing CSI faded. Her fantasy of being a Crime Scene Investigator wouldn't bring in money, only trouble, as Detective Tucker was so fond of pointing out. This energetic little lady wanted more cabinets and a breakfast bar in her kitchen and Jemma was eager to use her carpentry skills on something besides decks and porches.

"You don't live in Hickory Hills so this doesn't matter to you," Karen dropped her wrist and snapped her gum, "but Mrs. POA Windsor has started to make building a new home in our subdivision a nightmare. Just living near her sets my pulse racing like Junior Johnson with a load of moonshine, or like Ringo on steroids." She laughed at her own joke.

"Ringo Starr?" Jemma re-measured the space to re-direct attention to the work at hand. She chomped at the bit to get on with the task at hand. Carpentry and photography had been occupying her time during the ranch's off season, but she still managed to ride her horse Brandy most evenings.

"They were before your time. Come to think of it, they were before mine."

"What's a POA for anyway?"

"Property Owners Association. This one started at fifty dollars a year to plow the roads after snow storms and for re-graveling in the spring. We'd have a pot-luck lunch in the spring and a quick budget review in December. That was it."

"What changed?"

"When the original president died and the treasurer moved away three years ago, nobody wanted to do the little work that was involved, including me. We had a house plan review board but the only things we enforced were minimum square footage and no trailers. Later that was expanded to keep out modular homes. Petula agreed to be president and we were happy that someone cared enough to volunteer."

"And now? How did she get elected more than once if she's so hard to deal with?"

"Petula charms the men and talks of increasing home values. They love being on her board and don't miss a meeting. She's the only woman on the board, a mistake we women hope to remedy at the meeting coming up. She turned our friendly mountain into her own soap opera, starring herself. Maybe she was never in charge of anything before and this makes her feel powerful. Honey, even her husband stays out of her way in POA matters. He's never even attended a meeting since she took over. My guess is that things are calmer at home if he lets her loose on us. Of course I don't let my husband attend the meetings, either – our home is certainly calmer if he stays away. Anyway, lately she's been pushing for a special assessment of seven thousand dollars per owner to pave the road. That's a shopping trip to her but a lot of cash to most of us."

About twice that of her own savings account, Jemma thought. "The road is fine to me even with the couple inches of snow we got yesterday."

"Right, honey. She claims safety issues, as if the fire department or the sheriff couldn't travel almost as fast on the gravel we have. We have snow plowers on contract. Her latest focus is for houses in here to befit her image as mistress of the mountain." Karen emptied an ash tray with a single butt into the trash can. "My husband still has one after we cuddle, if you know what I mean."

Jemma nodded and tapped the paper with her pencil as a signal she wanted to get back to work. As she looked down at the tiny woman, she wondered if Karen knew her hair had a flat spot right on top.

"She's turned down Ann's plans again claiming they don't meet the square footage – but they do. The plans are for twenty-six hundred square feet and the POA minimum is for twenty-two hundred. She can't change the requirements until they are voted on at the meeting in two weeks." Karen opened the refrigerator and pulled out a diet soda. "Want one?"

Jemma shook her head. "The romance of living in these mountains includes live and let live, rugged individualism and all that. How does she get away with playing with people?" Jemma tugged on the flannel shirt she'd found in the men's section of the thrift shop. Blouse sleeves were always too short, same with pant legs.

"You've never met Petula Windsor, have you?" Karen poured the soda in a glass and took a big swallow.

"No, the name's not familiar." A development had to have a strong grapevine. Doing a good job for Karen could boost her reputation for carpentry work.

"Her husband is Ward Windsor, the Executive VP at Allgoode Bank. They moved to town fifteen or sixteen years ago. This'll be her third year as POA President. She's an agitator, likes to keep things stirred up. She treats us like we're her hive and she's queen bee. Honey, she'll get stung one of these days." Karen's eyes widened at her own pun, then she tittered. "Anyway, she complained about people dumping grass clippings and leaves in the woods behind their own houses, oh, and a man walking his dog on a leash before eight in the morning. Now she's bugging an owner wanting to build on the lot across the street. That's my friend, Ann. Come on, I'll show you."

Jemma gave up on rushing her customer. Karen led Jemma to a picture window in the living room, which had a view of the neighboring snow covered ridge through the leafless trees. That view could disappear if a house were built directly across the road. If the house were set to the left, though, where there was already a clearing, Karen would still see for miles.

"See where they've cleared the trees? Madam President even complained about that. She ran off the contractor and slapped a law suit on the owner. That law suit could cost the POA tens of thousands of dollars if it goes to court."

"Can't the other property owners do anything about her?"

"Short of murder?" Karen again snapped her gum. "I've been making good use of talking while shopping with some of the wives. Surprises may be coming Petula's way at the meeting."

"Whose property is it?" Jemma looked across the road at the lot and the relatively level spot for a house, an usual occurrence in the mountains.

"Ann Dixon, she was behind me at Watauga High by uh, a couple of years. "She always was a feisty little girl." Karen told Jemma about the June meeting.

"She knocked her down? A grown woman?"

"Petula would have called the police, but enough of us saw her grab Ann's arm – and the marks her nails left – that she didn't dare. I called it self-defense."

"So, the trouble-maker has met her match?" Jemma grinned, enjoying the mental image the China Doll up against the Mountain Woman on one of Alma's WWF TV shows.

"Not as a brawler. Ann owns Perfect for Framing, an art gallery in downtown Boone, she promotes local artists and photographers. One of her clients had a photo on the cover of Our State magazine."

"Photography." Jemma tapped the paper again. "I'll have to visit the shop. I take a few pictures myself." Great idea. She hadn't thought of putting her photographs up for sale anywhere besides the family guest ranch. Suppose her photos were seen by an influential person, a celebrity. Her reputation could grow, she could be asked to do photos for National Geographic or Atlantic magazines. She could be paid to travel...

"Yes, do visit the gallery. You'll like Ann, I promise." Karen glanced around as if just realizing she had been holding up the project. "Thank you for agreeing to build these cabinets on such short notice." Karen walked back to the kitchen. "Your Aunt Alma said you worked in the cabinet business before moving here."

"It's been a while since I've built anything requiring finesse but don't worry, it'll all come back to me." What was she thinking? Working with wood was her primary interest, or was it solving crimes? What happened to the application she'd submitted to the Watauga Sheriff's Department last week? How long does it take to process an application? When would she be called for an interview? Would Tucker, some called him her detective, give a good recommendation? Ti-ti-tat went her heart when she thought of him, even after three months of long phone calls and weekend dates.

"Are you sure?" Karen asked with a touch on Jemma's arm and Jemma realized she had been daydreaming. "Alma can be pretty persuasive."

"That she can be. But I can handle it, really. Alma said you wanted the new cabinets to match what you already have."

"That's right. These cabinets were custom-made when we built the house, and I love them. But now I want an island separating the work space from the eating area and a matching corner cabinet in that wasted space by the door, and the craftsman who made them isn't available."

"Are these antique glass for the corner cabinet?" Jemma knelt and examined two heavy panes of beveled glass leaning against the wall.

"Maybe not antique, but they are for the corner cabinet. Ann found them in the framing shop when she rented it. We were talking about what I'd like to do with this room and she gave them to me."

"She's a good friend."

"She certainly is, so it just makes me mad to see her treated this way by Ms Petula President." Karen snapped her gum and ran a hand down the door of one of the upper cabinets. "This is special heritage wood. Do you think you can get the same thing?"

Jemma pulled open one of the drawers and peeked underneath at the back of the drawer front. Oak with a clear finish was attractive and durable, but not hard to duplicate. The style was very plain, what some might call 'Shaker'. "I'm sure I can. I recognize it. The style is something I can handle too." Jemma cleared her throat. "If you want to think about it, I can come back another time. There's no obligation, just because you know Alma."

"No, no. I'm sure you'll do fine," Karen said without hesitation.

"When do you want me to start?"

"Now. Honey, the sooner the better. I want to have a celebration on December 31st."

"To ring in the new year?"

"More than that. I've invited the whole subdivision, excepting one or two, if you know what I mean. I've something in the works to stop Petula Windsor. Keep your fingers crossed."

Jemma drove the Blue Falls Ranch pickup out of Hickory Hills, the subdivision located three miles from Boone in North Carolina, and flipped up the heat dial to maximum on this clear cold day. She turned right onto the winding road that made it impossible to reach the fifty-five mile-an-hour limit even without the snow, drove around the mountain past neat rows of Christmas trees and turned right again onto a twisting, uphill gravel road.

She parked before an old cabin; her fingers reached for her camera before she thought. Stacked firewood took up one end of the covered porch. Icicles hung from the roof like fringe on a shawl of snow. Ahh, but she wouldn't invade the privacy of her aunt's friend. She put down the camera and left the warmth of the truck cab. Her boots crunched through the quarter inch of crust atop yesterday's snow. Each boot fall crackled like a bite into burnt toast. Crumbs of ice sparkled and scattered and slid down ahead of her sometimes careening off blades of dried grass or downed limbs poking above the white slope. She had only reached the first step when a white-haired, wrinkle-faced little woman came out to the top step vigorously motioning her inside. This was the eighty-seven year old widow Aunt Alma told her to visit?

"Come on in, child. It must be freezing out here."

Jemma ducked and followed her into the living room dominated by a wood stove. A low ceiling, well-worn furniture and eighty-degree heat greeted her. She unzipped her thick jacket and stuffed her gloves into the pocket. "This home was built in the early 1900s, wasn't it?"

Lottie Miller gestured to an overstuffed chair while she sat herself in an ancient rocker. "My daddy built it hisself. It war a wedding present for my momma. When they passed on, my Warren and I moved on in. He wasn't much taller than me so we didn't mind the low ceilings. Saw you flinch a mite when you came in." When Lottie smiled, her eyes almost disappeared into her cheeks.

"You don't miss much. At six feet, I automatically duck down. These six and a half foot ceilings are rare these days."

"Want some coffee? It'll only take a minute." Lottie grabbed the arms of her rocker, ready to pop up.

"No, thank you. I had plenty at Alma's earlier."

She kicked the floor to start rocking. "She called yesterday and said you was interested in my Warren's workshop tools?"

"Yes, ma'am. I hope this isn't too soon." And that the tools aren't worn out, she added silently.

"It's been nearly a year." Lottie looked down at her hands. "Alma said I got to do something about his shop." She glanced at Jemma then studied her old wedding band. "What did you have in mind?"

"I'm a cabinet maker without a workshop. When Alma told me that his tools and shop were collecting dust instead of sawdust, I thought about renting it."

Lottie let out a slow breath. "I was afraid you wanted to buy everything and move it. I'm not sure I could do that just yet." She giggled a bit. "Let's go on out to the shop. I reckon it'll be cold, so I best get my coat."

Jemma helped Lottie into her coat and followed her out the front door.

"My Travis shoveled the snow off this walk afore work this morning." A dozen mounted deer racks hung on the side of the shed, a horseshoe with the ends up was nailed above the door. "That's to keep evil away."

"I heard that a horseshoeing Catholic Saint held the devil captive until he agreed never to enter a place where a horseshoe was displayed."

"So that's where my story came from." Lottie gripped a metal handrail that trailed from the house to the workshop. "My Warren put in this railing for me a couple of years before he died." She opened the door and flipped on the lights. The fluorescent lights were dim, to be expected in cold weather.

Jemma walked the perimeter of the shop. A table saw and planer dominated one corner. Work benches held all kinds of toys from routers to air gun attachments to sanders. Jemma's heart beat fast but she merely said, "He used this shop a lot, didn't he?"

"Not so much in his last years."

Jemma nodded, playing the negotiation game. "Most of this is well over twenty years old. Mind if I try out some of it?"

Lottie went to the scrap wood pile, grabbed a piece and handed it to her. "Have at it. Take all the time you need. I'll be back where it's warm." She was out the door at once.

Jemma plugged in pieces of equipment and cut, sawed and drilled until she was satisfied that most of it still worked. It was worth well over five hundred a week to rent but she couldn't afford that much. She'd let her excitement at doing cabinet work get ahead of her sense, not for the first time.

Jemma knocked on the cabin door and welcomed the warmth after a half hour in the cold workshop.

Lottie joined her in the living room bearing a tray of hot tea and cookies. "Here, drink this. It'll warm your insides. I baked these molasses-oatmeal cookies yesterday." After setting down the tray, she added a couple of pieces of wood and a pinch of salt to the wood stove. "Keeps the ghosts away."

Jemma warmed her hands around the mug and sat. "How do you know Alma anyway?"

"Let me see. I guess I first met her at one of the places she used to cook at. But now, we talk regular at the UFO meetings."

"A sister believer." Jemma put down the mug, took off her jacket, and settled in a chair made for a short person. Jemma's knees were level with her chest. "She's careful not to miss one of those. Doesn't talk about them much."

17

Lottie handed Jemma a cookie on a saucer. "We studied on that. We got tired of people making fun of us so we decided to keep quiet about it. Did you see everything in the workshop?"

Jemma put her mug on the floor, balanced the saucer on her knees and bit into the cookie. "Mmmm, this is good. Competition for Alma."

Lottie beamed. "Mind if I tell her you said that?"

Jemma laughed. "Go ahead. She'll probably burn my toast in the morning. The belt sander didn't work but everything else seemed to. What would you charge for me to rent it on a weekly basis?"

"What's it worth to you?"

Jemma dusted the crumbs from her fingers and leaned forward. "A lot more than I can pay. To be honest, after I pay for the lumber, glue and other stuff, I'll be lucky to make five dollars an hour."

"Give me a dollar an hour and fix my back porch. Would that suit?"

"Yes, ma'am." Jemma gulped some tea. "That's generous. I didn't expect you to be that low."

"It'll be good to have the stuff be used. Warren would like it that way. It's not like I was selling it off or letting it go out of the family. This land, house, workshop, everything goes to my great grandson after I'm gone. It's important to keep land in the family, don't you think?"

"You're talking to someone who doesn't even own a car. I can see why it's important to you, though. This place has family memories." The house was almost claustrophobic to Jemma. Knicknacks, pictures piled one upon another, even a broken toy vied for space on the scarred table next to her chair. Too much stuff to be comfortable around, but live and let live.

"When you get older, you'll see the importance of things like carrying on the family name and keeping near the land. Enough of that. After you finish your cookie, we can look at the porch. You'll probably have to wait til Spring to fix it, but you can get an idea of the problem now. When do you want to start using the workshop?"

"Is tomorrow too soon?"

"Fine with me. Did you bring those pictures I told Alma I wanted to see? She's been bragging about your photography so much, I told her to have you show them to me."

Jemma stayed another twenty minutes with Lottie exclaiming over Jemma's photos of the horses at the ranch and the surrounding mountains and paused before opening the truck door. Sunlight streamed between the dormant trees creating a checkerboard of bright light reflecting off the snow and the tree shadows. She closed her eyes and faced the sun to absorb a little vitamin D. Drops of snow melt chimed as they hit the ice crust around her.

Chapter 2
THURSDAY

*D*ETECTIVE TUCKER CAUGHT himself doodling on his notepad instead of listening to the new sheriff discuss the changes in procedures. He should be grateful that he still had a job. Some folks were let go after the election. The sheriff had been talking non-stop for twenty minutes covering, word for word, the handouts in front of them.

"And now, on to personnel changes. As you know, a few people left the department with the outgoing sheriff. I'll be reviewing all personnel files for possible promotions and, in a few cases, dismissals. In view of the problems with the last administration, I wish to remind everyone that sexual harassment within the department is taken very seriously. What may seem mutual consent today may come back to haunt you. Think hard before fraternizing too closely with, ah, fellow officers of the opposite sex."

Tucker glanced at Graves, his partner of many years, who shook his head. Last week, Jemma had submitted her application to join the force. He'd been keeping company with her for a couple of months. She'd listed him as a reference, which put him between a cliff and a bear, either off the deep end or hugged to death. For the first time in his adult life, the stress of his demanding job faded when he was with someone. She even intruded in his mind when he worked. She talked about his job more than he did.

"What are you going to do?" Graves asked after the meeting.

"Beats me. I can't not recommend Jemma. CSI reruns are her favorite TV shows. Besides the fact that she'd chew me to the bone, she'd be hurt. I'd sooner stab myself in the heart than sabotage her dream." He was stuck, or likely would be in a few years when she would be promoted out of the communications department. She'd made it clear that she wanted to be an investigator, no matter where she had to start. She'd be carrying a gun, putting herself in dangerous situations. It's one thing to do it yourself and another to watch someone close go out each day and not know if she would be walking back in the door. Not that things were that serious between them. He stopped at a water fountain to ease the dryness in his mouth that happened whenever he thought of Jemma.

Tucker and Graves walked together to their desks in the new sheriff's complex. Moving from the old place to this one was relatively easy as far as Tucker was concerned. Parking was better; the jail cells were in a separate building; the lighting was brighter and he had more space. On the down side, all the desks were in one room; he had less privacy. So goes the life of a public servant, he thought as he dropped the pad on his desk and sat in his new swivel chair. He picked up a folder with the latest property damage case and put it back down. Maybe he'd work on the identity theft ones; they could be related. Three reports in one week constituted a crime wave in this rural county.

Graves leaned down and asked in a low voice, "Anything in your record I need to know about? They're reviewing all the files."

"Get out of here. You know everything there is to know about me."

"Do I?" Graves shot back as he left.

JEMMA STOMPED THE SNOW off her boots then entered the old two-story building where Perfect for Framing was located on a narrow side street in downtown Boone. The large paned windows facing the street let in lots of light. A bell tinkled above the glossy red door; the scarred wood floor creaked when she walked on it. On the wall to the right, an oversized painting of an aquarium hung with a small card stating "not for sale." Must be the owner's version of *feng shui* to ensure a prosperous business.

A lanky woman of fifty-something greeted Jemma. "Welcome to my place." She swept her arm in an arc, taking in the whole shop. "Have you been here before?"

"No. This is my first visit." Jemma liked the feel of the shop, the Queen Bees jazz playing in the background and the honest look of the owner. She'd photograph her in stark black and white, bringing out the angles of her cheekbones and jaw as well as the deep hollows of her eyes. It would not be a flattering portrait but a haunting study.

"I sell a wide variety of art and I do framing. Photographs are up in the mezzanine. I like to promote local artists and even have note cards created by some of them if you're looking for a small gift."

"You do?" Jemma reached into a shoulder bag and brought out a manilla folder. "I was wondering if you would take a look at these photographs."

"Sure. Let's lay them out over here at the counter. The lighting is better. I assume you're the photographer." She pulled glasses out of her blazer pocket. The blazer's patchwork design befitted a gallery devoted to artistic, hand-crafted items.

Jemma nodded, unzipped her own well-worn ski jacket and a fear-of-rejection lump formed in her throat.

"I'm Ann, by the way," the owner said as she put on her glasses and leaned over the counter to inspect each photo.

"I'm Jemma. Nice to meet you." A large photo of the owner in profile hung on the wall. The frame was ornate, contrasting with the simplicity of the face. A painted tiger signed by T. A. Strawser hung next to the profile. A painting of a murder of crows gathered in a tree top was propped in the window.

"You like horses, I see," Ann commented.

One of her favorite photos. "My parents own Blue Falls Ranch, down in Triplett. I lead trail rides and work part time as a carp ... er, cabinet maker."

Ann nodded but kept her gaze on the photographs. "I think we can carry some of these. I like the sun glinting off the cliff-side icicles, the horse and wrangler on the ridge at sunrise and the deer with her fawn. The amazing one of the turkey in flight." She straightened and took off the glasses. "I suggest you print them at eight by ten. I'll mat and frame them to eleven by four-teen. That's the most popular size. I keep forty percent and pay once a month. If you're trying to get rich off of this, I can't help you. What I can do is give you exposure."

"It's not about the money." Fame, maybe recognition would be a bonus. References would help, Jemma thought.

Ann nodded. "No need to explain, or even examine your motives, if you're that type of person. I know what it's like to have the urge to create and then the need to share it." She put the photos back in the folder and handed it to Jemma. "My late husband designed a house and I'm trying to get it built."

"That's creative in a big way. It's over in Hickory Hills, isn't it?"

Ann looked sharply at Jemma.

"I'm building the cabinets in your across-the-road neigh-bor's house. I overheard her talking about the POA president." Jemma tried on one of the hand-blown glass rings for sale in a bowl on the counter next to the register.

"President, my foot. Power-crazy pervert is more like it. I could strangle her. It's a wonder no one has killed her before this. What I don't understand is why she has it in for me – and for my late husband when he was alive. We'd never even met her before. When I bought the property, the seller was forced to pay eight thousand dollars in back POA dues. The real estate agent said the POA president was enthusiastic about the money. If she has her way, it will go toward having the main road paved, all the way up to the president's house at the top of the mountain."

"She's weird. I feel for you." Jemma liked this woman for her passionate outburst. "It has to be frustrating." She put the ring back in the bowl and tried on a second one with blue swirls the color of the winter sky.

"You don't know the half of it. My plans beat everything in the POA Bylaws. I've done all she's asked but she still won't sign off. She missed the approval deadline way back in June so I went ahead and had the septic and well dug. She ordered the contractor to stop but it was too late. At least I got that done before the ground froze up. "

Jemma forgot about the rings. "Then what happened?"

"She contacted the POA Board and talked them into suing me. When I talked to a lawyer, he said to settle out of court since the consent outweighed the timing, or something like that. I'm still thinking about it. Now it's winter and the ground's too hard to start the foundation." Ann pinched the bridge of her nose. "Plus, it's costing me a fortune to rent."

"What about the other committee or board members? What do they say?" She put that ring back and focused on Ann.

"My real estate agent can't get anyone else to answer the phone. She rules the rooster and the roost. It may have something to do with the fact that her husband has a big say at Allgoode Bank. There's a meeting coming up in two weeks and I plan to be there."

Jemma glanced at the mezzanine up the stairs. "Maybe she'll come to her senses. I'll be back later in the week and bring those prints. Thank you."

"Thank you for listening. I don't usually unload like that."

"It's a tough situation to be in." Jemma heard the door open. "Would you mind if I took a look at the photographs upstairs?"

"Please do. Your photos will be in good company. By the way, I'm having a Christmas party and would like for you to come and bring a friend."

Jemma nodded and listened to the details.

Ann turned her attention to the person coming in the door. "Hello, Flora. I was hoping you'd stop by today."

Jemma walked up the creaky, wooden stairs to the open loft area of the store. So many talented photographers in the Boone area – it was disconcerting. She couldn't help but overhear the conversation below.

"Ann, you were right. You did see my husband buy something from Saslow's Jewelers two weeks ago while you were in the mall. Here's the receipt." Flora's deep voice echoed off the walls.

"How did you get this?"

Flora applauded herself. "I searched his desk at the office while he and Petula were out to lunch one day last week. It wasn't hard to find. Whew, my hot flashes went into overdrive that day."

"A seven thousand dollar bracelet. You know, I had a hard time deciding to tell you about this. He may not be having an affair. Maybe he bought this for you and hasn't had a chance to give it to you."

"Not possible. It's gold and he knows I only wear silver. My skin reacts to the nickel in American gold. Don't you try to defend him. I know it's for Petula, emphasis on the first syllable, like 'petulant'." Flora's voice rose in pitch and volume.

Jemma strolled to the edge of the loft, pretended to study a photograph and watched the two women.

"Calm down. I'm on your side." Ann patted her friend on the shoulder. "Do you think she went after Darryl, you know, sexually, because you complained about her short working hours?"

"Working hours? She asked for a raise. She doesn't do anything even when she's there. I want her fired. And I want that bracelet." Her voice went from a climbing pitch to a low growl, all in one breath.

"You said you were allergic to gold." Ann waggled a finger at Flora.

"It doesn't matter. Now it's a trophy, a sign that Darryl sticks to me. Not her. It's proof that I beat her."

Jemma leaned over the railing as Flora jerked off her coat and pulled out a handkerchief.

"I hate menopause." She moped her face and neck. "I hate my ancestors for having heart problems. What I wouldn't give for the quick relief of hormones."

"What are you going to do now? Nothing drastic, I hope. You know how your temper's been on easy trigger these past couple of years."

"Look who's talking. You're the one who stabbed your own brother." Flora's brassy voice turned whiny as she wiped her face again.

"That was a long time ago. He survived. I survived by moving away for twenty years. We've both mellowed." Ann stared at her friend. "I keep my temper in check."

"I'm sorry to bring up that old stuff about your brother. I'm worried. I didn't mean to pick on you. I love Darryl and don't want a divorce. I won't get rid of him. Guess I'll have to get rid of her." Flora patted her face with the handkerchief.

They both laughed. Ann added, "Nice fantasy." Ann reached and touched the frame of the fish painting on the wall behind her. "We could frame her for something."

"Don't I wish," said Flora. "Something to take her mind off my Darryl."

"Something that will disgrace her."

JEMMA BOUNCED UP AND down in the driver's seat while waiting at a stop light in the older part of Boone. The lighted snowflake decorations on the street light poles sparkled even though it was daytime. The rearview mirror showed a line of cars with loaded ski racks. She grinned at the driver in the oncoming lane, causing him to do a double-take. For the umpteenth time, she wished she had a cell phone, even though Triplett valley was a dead zone as far as reception was concerned. Maybe someday she would commit to one. She'd love to call Tucker and tell him her photographs were going into an art gallery. On its own accord, her hand rubbed her heart as it went *ti-ti-tat*. Not that she could call him at the sheriff's department for something personal. Especially since she wanted to work there.

At Wal-Mart, Jemma loaded her disk of photos into the self service kiosk and paid with a credit card. The store was more crowded than usual because of holiday shopping. She'd have a little extra income by the time the statement arrived, thanks to cabinetry. Working with wood to make something beautiful as well as practical appealed to her sense of accomplishment. It was tangible, built with her own hands and brain. It would last for decades and house the food and utensils for preparing scrumptious meals. In contrast to the cabinets in her own place, which stored tools and clothes since she didn't cook and had no desire to learn. Alma's cooking at the ranch was way beyond Jemma's skills.

On the twenty-five minute drive home, she turned up the pickup's radio and sang along with the rock vocals. The first switchback curve down Elk Creek Road, just past the Blue Ridge Parkway bridge, toned down her celebration. The view through the skinny, sucked-in-for winter trees showed three rows of brown ridges. Nestled between two of those ridges was home, Blue Falls Ranch. The steering wheel shook when she took the corner too fast, swerving into the other lane. Downshifting, she regained control of the truck. The last thing she needed was to spin out on black ice. Long skinny icicles hung from a rocky outcrop on the uphill side of the road.

What if she'd gone off the road at that curve without a guard rail, if a car had been coming uphill, or worse yet, if Tucker had seen her drive like that? She turned off the music and slowed, glancing to the left – then she hit her brakes.

An open cardboard box sat amidst discarded beer cans on the overlook. Had she seen movement inside the box? It was big enough for a medium sized dog. She glanced at the clock. The

Humane Society would be closed at this hour.

She backed into the oncoming lane since she could see no one was ahead coming up hill, swerved onto the shoulder and cut the engine.

The sturdy box moved when she approached and squatted down. "There's nothing to be afraid of," Jemma said, hoping to soothe the animal. Expecting to be greeted by a bark, Jemma sucked in her breath when two sets of golden eyes blinked at her. Cats. What did she know about cats?

"Now what?" she asked them. They crowded together at the back of the box, one black and one gray. "I can't leave you here. Tell you what, I'll take you to my place until I can get you to the Humane Society. Will that suit you?" She could almost hear Bo grumble about feeding horses, dogs, birds and now cats. The ranch had cats, but they were feral and kept down the mice in the barn.

Jemma put the box in the passenger seat and buckled it in. They were older than kittens but not yet adult cats, she thought as she snapped a couple of pictures. "Adolescent" suited their current age – or maybe "teenage kitties." She had to drive a quarter mile down the road before finding a drive big enough for her to turn around and go back up the mountain. Some people were so mean to animals. Do they think the woods is a safe place to dispose of them? How hard was it to take them to a shelter or a vet's office? Someone had failed to have their pet neutered and then wouldn't deal with a litter.

A quick trip to Food Lion and she had a litter box, litter, dry and wet food and a cat toy that a customer in the store suggested she get.

"You guys are so lucky," she said to the kitties on the drive to the ranch. "I had a few dollars left in my wallet." She caught glimpses of them while navigating the switchback curves even though they stayed huddled in a corner of the box. Gradually, on the three mile descent, snow in the woods was less and less and disappeared completely. At the bottom of the mountain, she took Elk Lane past the gray, stringy kudzu vines looped into and across trees like they tied the trees to the ground. She watched carefully since early shadows in the deep valley hid the dogs and deer that also traveled the road.

Once she turned into the driveway at the Blue Falls Ranch, she saw two dozen trail horses huddled around hay bales near the barn. She spotted Brandy, her mare, up against Handsome. Although the ranch was open all year, most of their winter customers were more interested in skiing than riding. Brandy raised her head and nickered when Jemma drove by the corral. Even without the kitties, she wouldn't have had time for a ride today.

Jemma took the box and groceries to her cabin. First thing, she closed the door to the upstairs. It wouldn't do for kitties to explore her newly finished office and library. She'd heard about cats' claws and books. "This is only temporary but it's better than out in the cold," she told the kitties as she set their box down in the bathroom. She fixed the litter box and set out canned cat food, dry food and water. The cats didn't come out.

She figured she'd give them some privacy, besides she was getting hungry herself.

As she approached the main lodge, a dust devil twirled the dried leaves up into the air higher than the two-story structure. The back porch chimes clanged, scattering the winter-pale gold-finches from the feeders.

"How'd it go this morning?" Alma asked when Jemma walked into the ranch kitchen.

Jemma smacked a big kiss on her cheek then stole a hush puppy from the pile Alma had just cooked. "You're the best. Thank you, thank you. I'll never snicker at the mention of your UFO meetings again. I promise." She blew on the hot cornmeal concoction before popping it into her mouth. Alma awarded her with a swat on the hand when she reached for another.

"Humph. That good?"

"Better. Lottie's letting me use her shop for not much more than the electric will cost her."

29

Alma emptied the last basket of fried cornmeal and turned off the deep fat fryer. "I been knowing her for, well, a long time. She'll like the company so be sure to visit her every day you work there, young lady." Alma held Jemma's gaze for a moment for emphasis.

"I will, but not for long. I don't have a lot of time." Besides, what would she talk about, she questioned silently. UFOs were fantasy.

"Ten, fifteen minutes will do. Hand me that bowl from the top shelf, will ya? What about Karen? Will you be able to build what she wants?" Alma took the bowl from Jemma and dumped in the cole slaw she'd made earlier.

"Thank goodness she has a log house. She wants a simple design of solid wood, polyurethane only. It won't be beyond my skill level. But there's more."

Alma took the slow cooked pork barbecue from the oven.

Jemma's mouth watered. A friend who was a real estate broker had cooked up a dozen Boston butts in his outdoor gas drum cooker and sold Alma a couple. Jemma picked up the basket of hush puppies and bowl of cole slaw and followed her aunt through the swinging door into the dining hall.

"What's more?" Alma asked while arranging the food on the side board.

"Karen told me about Perfect for Framing, an art gallery, that carries photographs by local artists. Those photos you wanted me to show Lottie? I showed them to the owner. She liked them."

"That's great." Alma returned to the kitchen for the bottles of vinegar-based sauce Dan had mixed up and took them out to put on the tables.

Jemma followed and helped distribute the bottles. "I went to Wal-Mart, had bigger copies printed and plan to sign them today. All due to you."

"Glad to help."

Jemma set the last bottle in place. "Guess what else?" Before Alma could say anything, Jemma said, "I have kitties." Jemma told her about the box by the road while they finished preparing for the supper guests.

"By the way, the sheriff's department called. I told them you could be there for an interview in the morning. Hope that'll fit your busy schedule."

Jemma gulped. "No sense putting it off." Interview. Tomorrow. What to wear? What to say? A chance to work near Tucker and to see him every day. *Ti-ti-tat*. Would that be good or the end of their new relationship? Lots of couples can't work together and have enough sense not to try. She could be near him and feel his breath when he spoke to her instead of imagining his face across the county on the other phone. She did wonder about the women in the office. Did they flirt with him or make snappy comebacks to his comments? Not that she was worried.

The door opened and a small crowd came in, wranglers, some neighbors, skiers and a few non-skiing customers. "Listen up everyone," Alma called out. "The Boone Christmas parade is day after tomorrow. It has fire trucks, antique cars, Red Hat ladies, Boy Scouts, wagon trains, dancers, bicycles and horses. I know it can't compete with sliding down a ski slope but it is a lot of fun."

Jemma told her news about the photographs and reveled in the applause. Then she talked about the kitties, asked if anyone knew who had left them and did anyone want them.

Chapter 3
FRIDAY

*T*HE KITTIES HAD USED the litter box and eaten during the night but Jemma hadn't seen them before leaving. She didn't have time to take them to the Humane Society today, maybe tomorrow. After the morning interview at the sheriff's office, Jemma drove the pickup to Lowe's Hardware and picked up wood and hardware for the breakfast bar. Even at the hardware store, holiday crowds created long lines at the checkout counters. The interview had gone well so she tried to dismiss it from her mind. Even her wide-ranging interests were viewed as a positive because she could relate to a variety of people and situations. As Alma had instructed, Jemma visited with Lottie for a few minutes. Most of the snow had melted. Once in the workshop, she changed from her dressy blouse and pants and into work clothes, remembering to put her good clothes in the truck to keep off sawdust. The rest of the morning flew by while she cleaned and rearranged the tools and tables, setting the shop up to be her own space. Lottie came in and offered her dinner. Jemma had packed her lunch, but welcomed the opportunity to eat at Lottie's kitchen table. Travis, Lottie's great-grandson, was already at the table, but stood when Jemma came in the back door. He came home most days for a home-cooked meal, Lottie said. Tall as Jemma and lean, Jemma figured his shoulders and chest would fill out soon if he kept eating Lottie's cooking. His eyes, like Lottie's, almost closed when he smiled.

Maybe one day she could photograph the two faces, cheek to cheek, in natural evening light, as a study in genetics. Same eyes, nose, same face shape. Even the skin tone had similar hues, hers mellowed, his vibrant.

He sat immediately when Lottie put a steaming bowl of chicken stew on the table in front of him. "Yes, ma'am, I try to keep Mamaw here straight but fail mightily, I'm afraid." Travis hunched over and corralled the bowl with his right arm and dug in.

"Sure you don't want some? I made plenty of this Peel-a-Pound Chicken soup." Lottie held the ladle above the heavy pot on the stove and licked her lips.

"I don't want to take advantage of you. You've been so good to me about the tools and such."

Lottie ladled some into a bowl and set it in front of Jemma. "That skinny sandwich of you'rn won't last half the afternoon. I send one that size along with Travis here for a late afternoon snack. He works at that Ford place sometimes until seven at night."

"Not often, Mamaw. Most of the time I'm back here shortly after five-thirty. I'm good about punching that time clock exactly on time." Travis bit into a piece of cornbread.

"What do you do at the Ford place?" Jemma spooned some soup into her mouth. The green beans, tomatoes and cabbage were almost as good as Alma's. She swallowed and dipped her spoon for more.

"I'm a mechanic. I factory trained in Charlotte, worked off the mountain for a couple of years, then transferred up here from Hickory last summer."

"He's working toward being a Senior Master Technician. When he finishes nearly six hundred hours of training, they send him on a cruise. He's promised to take me. I never been to the

Cari-be-an." Lottie finished seeing to everyone else's needs and sat at the table.

Jemma smiled at Travis. "Neither have I. All that training must take a long time. I'm impressed."

Travis paused in eating and sat up straighter. "I've scheduled the classes as tight as I could so's I won't have to leave Mamaw once I'm finished."

Lottie's eyes disappeared in her proud smile. "He moved in here just in time to help me with the canning. Those carrots and cabbage, even the green peppers came from my garden. I froze a bunch of this soup in the fall so we'd have some home grown vegetables this winter."

"It's delicious. It can't be easy growing a garden in these mountains." Jemma ate another spoonful of soup, glad the cabbage didn't overwhelm the other flavors.

"My garden's shrunk over the years but I still grow enough to keep me and one or two others until the next crop comes. Years back, we collected walnuts from the trees over the ridge. Not now. Those land-grabbin' Windsors cut them down to build a guest house big enough for two families. What a waste. Lord, if my freezer were to conk out, I don't know what I'd do, what with the cost of appliances these days."

"Don't fret about the Windsors, Mamaw. I'm biding my time. She'll bite her own tail one of these days." Travis patted his Mamaw on the shoulder before taking in another piece of cornbread.

"Waste of time. Stay away from her." Lottie swatted Travis with a dishtowel.

Jemma broke the strain that had come into the conversation. "Down on the ranch, we lose power a few times every winter. Last time, we had a pine snap off eight feet from the ground and just miss a power line. What about here?"

"My freezer's out on the back porch where it stays cold enough even without power for a couple days. The Blue Ridge Electric crews cleared in this area in the fall. It's been a long five years since the last time they trimmed all the trees near the electric lines. Have you seen that giant two-foot saw on an extension pole? Lawd, it can cut limbs high as the barn roof."

"They cart around a chipper, too," said Travis. "No one has to clean up after them."

Travis finished his meal and stood. "Gotta go, Mamaw. Nice to meet ya, Jemma." He put on a lined jean jacket over his uniform, grabbed a cookie from the jar on the counter and took a bite as he left. "Gotta head back to work."

"Same here." Jemma carried her bowl to the sink. "Thank you. I don't want you thinking you have to feed me when I'm here. I appreciate it but I'm in your debt already."

"I hear you. Don't fret. I understand. Now, shoo. Let me get to my work and you get to you'rn."

Jemma, in winter coat and work gloves, carried in the wood and hardware in a few trips from truck to workshop. The two by fours she'd picked out for the frame were straight, she'd made sure of that. The small wood stove in the corner took off the chill in the large space. It was far from warm but perfect for physical labor. The top frame of the peninsula bar was larger than the base since it would support an extended eating area. She screwed in the upright supports to the base, then attached the upper frame. At this point it was a big open rectangular box.

Karen's bar stools were standard size, thirty-four inches tall, so Jemma double checked the bar's box height of forty inches, leaving a two inch depth for the counter top. She put the level on each side to make sure the whole box wasn't cockeyed. Karen had four bar stools so the bar was long, leaving thirty inches for each stool plus extra room on the end. So far, all she'd used was her own screw gun and the chop saw. Jemma looked around the workshop. Next time would be more fun, she thought as she swept up the sawdust and deposited it in a trash can by the door.

THAT AFTERNOON TUCKER GATHERED his badge, adjusted his holster and gun and slipped on his jacket, all the while glancing at the clock. He drank the last of the water in his coffee cup, his way of cutting back on coffee. Why hadn't Jemma called to tell him about her interview with the Communications Chief? He'd been out when she finished the interview and the chief wasn't talking. He and Graves walked out the front door of the new Watauga County law enforcement complex.

"Break-in at a home in Hickory Hills," Graves said, checking the notes on his clipboard. "It happened while both residents were at work this morning. Mrs. Petula Windsor came home for lunch and found her husband's study a wreck. She called him, then us. She asked for a detective, not a patrolman."

Tucker drove. "Mrs. Windsor knows something about our system. That makes an even dozen cases for me. What about you?"

"I'm up to fifteen but aim to close a couple this week."

"I hope the traffic isn't too bad at New Market Center." Tucker left off the siren as the patrol car wound through the congested Boone streets, onto scenic Highway 194, then onto Meat Camp Road. Christmas tree farms, occasional pines and rhododendron slicks added green to the dark forests. Snow lingered in the higher elevations. Cow trails cut into the steep hillsides towering above the narrow road. Hickory Hills was tucked back into a hollar and had a curvy road that led to the top of the mountain. In the summer, the homes were hidden. Now, the red or green rooftops popped out of the brown tree hillside. "Which one is it?"

"The one at the top."

Chunks of icy snow lined the road, leftover from plowing earlier in the week. The circular drive in front of the house was paved with red brick. "Must be five thousand square feet in that house." Tucker slowed and parked the car, taking in the stone facade, the two wings off the main house, the two chimneys, the many roof lines, and even a guest house down a walking path to the right – seemed to Tucker that much building in the mountains meant somebody had more money than sense. An empty man-made pond and fountain had been winterized. Mulch-covered swaths surrounded the pond with a gazebo strategically situated for the best view. He pushed the button beside the massive carved wood door and heard a gong sound deep in the house.

The woman who opened the door was a looker – blond, skinny, but she seemed a tad overdone to Tucker as well. Her icy blue dress matched her eyes – or maybe she had contact lenses to match her dress.

"Mrs. Windsor, I'm Detective Tucker and this is Detective Graves." He resisted the urge to bow. Department policy said to use first names, but that would be awkward with this one.

"Do come in, officers. My husband is in his study now. Please call me Petula." Her heels clicked on the slate floor in the entry way but were silent as she led them on thick carpet to the study. "I was shocked, shocked I tell you, when I came home to this intrusion."

"What time was that, ma'am?" Graves asked.

Petula stopped at the study's open door. She checked her watch. "It must have been an hour ago. Normally, I leave work in Boone at noon, come home for a bite to eat and a moment of peace and quiet, then like to be back around two. I was late today. I had a flat tire on the way home and had to wait for Triple-A. After all that, imagine coming home to a scene like this." She pointed a manicured fingernail to a room the size of Tucker's whole house.

A man, Mr. Windsor, sat in a leather armchair in front of the windows studying the scene before him. He glanced up, but remained seated while the detectives crossed the room.

Floor to ceiling bookshelves rose to the twelve-foot ceilings. Leather-bound books were neatly arranged with figurines interspersed. The only lived-in part of the room was the oversized wood desk dominating one side. Tucker took in the open desk and file cabinet drawers, files strewn around, a skewed lamp-shade distorting the light and an office chair backed against the wall. The husband rose, leaned in and held out his hand. Late fifties, beefy face, probably a drinker by the spider veins on his cheeks and nose. Too many business dinners.

"I'm Ward Windsor. Thank you for coming." The large man dressed in an expensive suit shook both their hands.

Deep voice, Yankee, Tucker thought. Much older than his wife.

"What's missing?" Detective Graves asked.

"Petula, would you make these men some coffee?" Ward squared his shoulders.

After a long pause, she raised one eyebrow, nodded and left the room.

Ward led them to the drawer side of his desk and nodded toward an open drawer. "I keep this drawer locked all the time. It usually has around two thousand in cash and an old thirty-eight special. The maid service knows to leave this desk area alone. Petula seldom comes in here."

"Why lock it?" Tucker asked while checking out the gouges in the drawer face. Probably a flathead screwdriver or a small pry bar.

"Old habit from living up north. I don't like to tempt fate. But this time, I had a report in there. A very personal report. One that I hate to even mention, but need to. You see, I've had a private investigator following my wife." Ward sunk down into the tooled leather seat of the executive chair. "He took pictures, disturbing photos. She doesn't know about this."

"Was she seen with another man?"

Ward nodded. Worry lines deepened in his fleshy face.

"Someone you know?"

"Her boss." Ward stroked his tie and squared his shoul-ders. "He's also a client, I'm Vice President of Allgoode Bank in Boone."

"Mind if we contact your PI and get a copy?" Tucker went

to school with one of the two private investigators in Boone and had had good dealing with this one.

Ward rubbed his face, then looked straight at Detective Tucker. "Why not? I'll call my investigator and let him know you're coming. No telling what I'd do if I saw Darryl Johnson right now. You might also want to talk to Ray, Raymond Viccaro, Petula's brother."

"Why's that?" Tucker wrote down the lead.

"He's mentioned in the report. The money's missing and he knows that I keep some in here." The phone rang, Ward picked it up, then slammed down the receiver. "Another hang up,"

Tucker's attention picked up at a potential complication in the case. "Another?"

"It happens once or twice a day. The caller ID shows that the number's blocked."

Petula returned pushing a cart loaded with coffee, cookies and nuts. After a flurry of passing out the coffee, she sat in a nearby chair and looked at Tucker expectantly.

"Was anything else missing or disturbed?" Tucker asked, holding the delicate coffee cup and saucer in his hand. Petula's face showed little emotion, no frown of concern, no raised eyebrow. Her face seemed somehow frozen.

"The files on my desk are tossed around. I haven't touched anything except for this chair. Did you change anything, Petula?" Ward barely looked at his wife.

"No. As soon as I saw it, I called you. My POA notes are still on the desk. I'm the President but I still want my husband's support on important issues, you understand." Petula stood and glided to the French doors. "They must have come in here. This door was open about an inch. I did close it to keep the heat in. Oh, dear, I guess I shouldn't have done that." Petula's hand fluttered to her throat.

The gesture smacked of theatrics. Tucker glanced at Graves. Graves said, "That's all right, ma'am. The prints should still be on the outside, if that's the way the intruder came in."

"Does anyone else live here? Do you have a maid?" Tucker didn't mind looking at Petula.

"Of course we have a cleaning service. They were here yesterday." Petula returned to her seat and crossed her legs at the ankle.

A fleeting look of impatience crossed Ward's face. "No one else lives here, Detective."

Tucker said, "We'd like to look over the room. Would you mind leaving us to our job and take the cart with you? This will take a while, so you can return to work." They returned the cups and saucers to the cart and watched the duo leave.

"It looks straightforward enough." Graves clipped the pen to his clipboard and looked around, careful not to touch anything.

"Good. I wouldn't mind a simple one for a change. Petula's flat tire bothers me, though." Tucker retrieved the camera and dusting kit from the trunk of the car and the two documented the scene. Only two clear sets of prints showed up, probably the Windsors', but Tucker would process them anyway.

Later, Tucker and Graves stopped by the private investigator's office and picked up a copy of the Windsor report in a dark gray folder embossed with a silver shield. They parked and scanned it and the photos. They may have been shocking to Ward but Tucker'd seen worse. Petula's body was as taut as her face. The man's body reminded him of a washed-out pumpkin left in the field too long.

Tucker said, "It'd be faster to go to his office than bring him in like we'd rather do."

"Your call. The surprise visit might scare him into telling more."

Tucker drove, parked, and was greeted at the Star Lite Properties office by none other than Petula, receptionist. "I work here part time, mostly to keep busy," she explained without being asked. She didn't seem surprised to see the detectives.

"We'd like to see Darryl Johnson," Detective Tucker said, the report tucked under his arm. He noted that the spacious, upscale area emphasized the commercial side of the real estate business rather than the home sales portion. Modern straight chairs didn't invite lingering as a living room setting would. Brochures on the table were of commercial properties.

Petula led them to her boss' office and returned to her desk.

Detective Tucker closed the door before addressing Mr. Johnson, who was covering a dark gray folder with other files. "I'm Detective Tucker and this is Detective Graves and we'd like to ask you a few questions." Mr. Johnson stood: thinning hair, moderate belly under a custom blazer, Floridian. He looked better fully dressed. An LCD monitor on the cadenza behind him pictured an MLS business listing. The large green leaves on a tall potted plant in the corner shone as if waxed.

"The name's Darryl," he said while shaking hands. His brows furrowed. "What about?"

"A break-in and a copy of this report, " Detective Tucker reached on the desk and pulled out the dark gray folder from under a stack of papers, "was stolen. Want to tell us about it?"

"I, uh, this report was on my desk when I came back from lunch today. I swear. I knew nothing about it until today." His gaze darted from one detective to another. A fleeting smirk marred the performance.

"Want to comment about the contents?" Tucker opened the folder to verify that the report and photos were the same. The naked bodies gleamed and shimmered for all to see.

Darryl shook his head, then reconsidered. He gestured for the detectives to take seats before lowering himself into his leather armchair and closed the folder as if to hide his deeds. "I love my wife, I really do. She's borne and raised our four children. She's a wonderful, caring woman."

"I understand, but ..." Tucker left the sentence dangling, hoping to hear how and why he'd stolen the report.

"But we've been together thirty years and, well, I'm not getting any younger. When Petula showed some interest in me – as a man – I thought I'd see what else was out there. Typical of men my age, I guess. My first and only affair and I got caught." His self-depreciating smile was practiced. "Nothing serious. We got together a few times."

"At her guest house?"

Darryl nodded. "She suggested it. To be honest, it was thrilling the first time. After that, I started thinking about my marriage and Flora. She's developed a temper, and is going through changes, but I still consider her my best friend. I bought Petula a bracelet as a way to say 'Thanks, but no thanks,' if you know what I mean."

"When was this?"

"A couple of weeks ago. I broke it off earlier this week."

"Is that when these photos were taken?" Tucker held up two of the photographs by the corners.

Darryl flinched when he looked at the photos. "'One last time,' she said."

Tucker slid the pictures back into the folder on the desk. "How did Petula take the break-up?"

Darryl cleared his throat. "She was hurt, of course, but she didn't cry or anything like that. We weren't serious."

"Does Petula know about the report and photos?" Tucker asked, letting Graves concentrate on note taking and observing.

"I haven't mentioned it to anyone. Like I said, the folder was on the desk when I returned from lunch."

"Where were you today between eight and one?" Keep it simple, tell the truth, Tucker silently coached.

"I came in around eight, left around ten to look at some property the owner wanted listed, had lunch at Boone Drug, then came back here around one."

He recited his itinerary without emotion, almost with rehearsed authority.

"What's the property owner's name?"

"No one was home. He dropped off the key yesterday so I checked out the house alone." Darryl straightened in his chair. "I guess that means that I don't have an alibi."

Detective Graves nodded. "And the stolen property was on

your desk."

"Anyone could have put it there. We always have an agent here during lunch but they could have been on the phone or making coffee and not seen someone come in the front door."

"We'll keep this evidence." Tucker picked up the folder, mindful of fingerprints.

"Please," Darryl said, rising slowly, "don't tell my wife about this."

"She won't hear about it from us. It might be a good idea for you to tell her about it since she's your best friend and all," Graves said.

"My reputation in the community affects real estate sales. I could contribute to the Police Fund." Darryl reached for his wallet in his back pocket.

Tucker rose slowly and stared at him, not believing the implications.

"No, of course not. Let me take you to lunch."

"Darryl, that hole you are digging is deep enough."

Chapter 4

*T*UCKER DROVE AND GRAVES read the log on the way to the Ford dealership. Traffic stalled as one of the eight elementary schools let out and busses as well as cars jockeyed for position on 421 around New Market Center. The sole county high school would be relocating a mile down the highway. As far as Tucker knew, traffic control solutions had yet to be addressed. Why the twenty thousand people of Boone and the additional thirty thousand in the county wouldn't elect more forward-thinking commissioners was beyond Tucker's comprehension.

"The PI followed Petula for only two days before taking the photos with Darryl. On the log, she had met with her stepbrother and had an animated discussion at the coffee shop. I wish he could have heard what they talked about."

"And make our jobs easier?" Tucker parked and they met Raymond Viccaro in the entrance to his sales cubicle. Empty candy wrappers lay on top of a pile of well-thumbed Car and Driver magazines. Papers and forms littered his desk.

"I'm Ray. What type of car are you looking for?"

As Tucker introduced himself, he noted Ray, medium build,

trim with a small paunch, had lots of hair and was around fifty. "We'd like to talk to you about something else."

Ray circled around his small desk and remained standing. "Sure, what is it?" He tapped a pen between his thumb and forefinger.

Detective Graves said, "We've had a break-in and want to know what you can tell us about it."

"What was broken into?"

"Your brother-in-law's study. Where were you between eight and one this morning?"

Ray widened his eyes and dropped the pen onto his desk. "Ward's study? I was right here. Check with anybody." He tugged on his belt and rested his hands on his hips.

"Tell us about your day, from the time you got up until right now." Tucker leaned against the cubicle wall and it swayed.

"Let me see. It was slow so I walked around the parking lots to check some details on the new cars. I like to have a visual image of what I'm selling. You sure you don't need to trade up to something? I have some special deals running right now." Ray reached to a plastic wall pocket and held up a brochure.

"Not now. And then what?"

He let the brochure drop back into its tray. "I talked with a 'not now' customer and let him take a test drive. Then it was noon. Are you driving your personal car right now? I could take a look and give you a good trade in price."

"Can anyone verify where you were?" Annoying and bold enough to try to make money off an officer on duty, Tucker thought. Maybe we should have made him come to the complex and interviewed him on our turf.

"Some of the shop mechanics may have seen me walking around. The counter clerk saw me with the customer. Say, maybe you can help me. Someone's been messing with my office here. Do you think these crimes are related?"

"What's missing?"

"Nothing is missing but my papers get moved around, girly magazines appear, cartoons are tacked up on my bulletin board.

Letters to the editor about my sister show up on the coffee room board. One time, someone put a sticker on my car that said 'Honk if you think I'm ugly.'"

Graves smiled.

"It wasn't funny when I had to spend an hour getting that sticker off." Ray stepped out of the cubicle. "Come on, I'll take you to the clerk."

Ray introduced the detectives and asked the clerk behind the plexiglass window, "You saw me with that customer this morning, didn't you? Big guy, bib overalls, scraggly beard?"

"First thing this morning. You handed him some dealer plates," she said.

Her voice was distorted by the glass, similar to the setup at the sheriff's complex. "Did you see Ray any other time?"

"It's hard to say. I don't keep tabs on the sales people, you know? They're all in and out a lot."

"Thank you," Detective Tucker said, then returned to Ray's office. "Your timing's a bit different from hers. You said you walked the lot first and then dealt with the customer."

Ray tapped his head. "A little too much to drink last night. I got things turned around."

"That's all for now. We may need your official statement later."

JEMMA UNLOCKED HER CABIN door and crept inside. No one greeted her. She checked the kitties' food bowls – they were empty. "Here kitty, kitty," she called as she searched the living room for them. She entered the bedroom and saw a lump under her comforter. "Who is that under there?" she asked, surprised that her voice had taken on a sing-song lilt. She knelt and lifted the comforter until she saw it was the black one. "You're my undercover kitty." Jemma scooped up the cat and held it close, cooing and petting it until it stopped shivering.

"There's nothing to be afraid of, little one." She lifted its tail. "Ah, a little boy and you've been fixed. Someone took good care of you. Your eyes are so golden, why did they give you up?"

A meow came from the corner of the room. Jemma put the black one on the bed and he dove back under the covers. Jemma cornered the gray one, hugged it to her chest, then checked and found it was female. "I've got to go, little girl. I'll put you with your brother."

Jemma stopped in the ranch kitchen to see if Aunt Alma needed help.

"Naw, I can manage. With only eight skiers and the ranch hands and us, this is easy work for me. I kinda like being in charge while your parents are on that cruise." Alma picked up another potato and scrubbed it. "I'm having pan fried trout, spicy orange beets and scalloped potatoes, all from Jane's *Mountain Born and Fed* cookbook. Tell me about the interview."

"The only opening they have is in communications so I talked to the Chief of Communications. It went well enough. Dispatchers rotate between night and day shift. There's training involved."

"I don't know that I like you driving Elk Creek Road that often at night."

"Aunt Alma?" Jemma regretted her wail as soon as she said it. "Sorry."

"I know you think you're all grown up but to me, you're still my concern. Anyway, I get all those police types mixed up."

"Each department answers their own calls. There's the Town of Boone Police, the Appalachian State University police, the Emergency section that answers when you call nine-one-one, and then there's the Watauga County Sheriff's Department. I'm interested in the sheriff's department."

Alma paused and added another potato to the pile. "Are there benefits?"

"They have insurance, retirement, accrued vacation and sick days, all the stuff government workers have. It would be forty hours a week."

"Did they bring up the DUI?" Alma resumed scrubbing but not peeling the potatoes.

"I did. I didn't want to hide anything. She said that it was a while ago and asked me about my current habits." Jemma spied the salt and pepper shakers on the table, retrieved the bulk containers and began filling the shakers with fresh spices.

"Did you mention that you're keeping time with Detective Tucker?" Alma asked remaining bent over the sink and scrubbing away.

Ti-ti-tat. Would there ever come a day when her heart didn't react to his name? "She already knew that. If and when I advance, I could never work under the same supervisor. Since we are already 'keeping time,' sexual harassment charges are not an issue."

Alma aimed the scrub brush at Jemma. "Well, child, do you think you got the job?"

Jemma nodded. "The interview went well. I like the Communications Chief. The money is fine. I should hear something within two weeks. With Christmas and the holidays, I wouldn't start until the New Year."

"You don't sound too excited."

Jemma finished with the salt and pepper and placed the shakers on a tray. "It's not that. My mind is on the breakfast bar I'm building. I should be able to construct the four drawers and make the cabinet doors tomorrow. After that, I'll be able to start on the top. I found some beautiful white oak to work with." Jemma smiled to herself, remembering almost tusseling with a contractor over those pieces of wood.

"Do you still have the kitties?"

"Yeah. They're scared." A tender spot in Jemma's heart opened.

Alma moved to the cutting board to slice the potatoes. "I could take them to the Humane Society in the morning."

Jemma caught her breath. "They're my responsibility. If I don't have time tomorrow, I'll do it next week. No rush." Not willing to think about the future of the kitties, Jemma looked around the kitchen for something else to do.

"It's an hour before supper. Did you get to visit with Brandy today?"

"No, I'll head that way right now."

Brandy *nickered* as Jemma approached her in the pasture. Brandy stood near Handsome and Visa. It wasn't yet cold enough to keep blankets on them but a chill was in the still air. "Hey, girl, miss me?" Jemma asked, then patted the long face. "Do you feel like a short ride? Maybe I can get Bo to go with us."

Wranglers Bo and Miguel grabbed saddles as soon as Jemma suggested a ride. Wayne still had chores to do. Jemma needed the exercise as much as the horses did. The wranglers filled in Jemma on the events of the day and she told them about the kitties.

"Are you getting used to us?" Jemma asked Miguel, who had replaced a wrangler determined to make it on the rodeo circuit.

"Yes, ma'am. Fine horses." He still didn't look her in the eye.

"I hope that bunk house isn't too noisy at night. I understand Bo's quite a snorer."

"Not so bad as Wayne." Miguel ducked his head.

Bo scowled. "Wait till spring when we bring in more crew. We issue ear plugs."

"What are they?"

"You'll find out." Bo dropped the reins and momentarily stuck his fingers in his ears. "There was a break-in over at Hickory Hills today."

Jemma shook her head. "You're addicted to that police scanner." Jemma breathed in the chilly air and patted Brandy's neck, glad to be with her.

"Aw, come on, Jemma, you're just as nosy as I am."

Jemma laughed. "I'll bite. What happened?"

"It was this morning, at the house at the top of the mountain in the development. See if you can find out any details from your detective."

"He's not *my* detective." Jemma clicked Brandy into a trot and then into a run, loving the wind on her face and the rhythm of Brandy's gait. The wranglers followed her lead. If Tucker really were hers, would that tingle of excitement disappear from too much exposure? Right now, right there, she wanted to possess him, to keep him near her, to have him focus only on her. Wild, politically-incorrect thoughts beat in her head in time to Brandy's galloping hoofs. Hers. All hers. At her fingertips whenever she wanted him, wanted his attention. Hers to indulge in and overdose on. Sanity returned; a person never could possess someone else. She wouldn't like it if Tucker became possessive and jealous of her every move that didn't involve him.

"Miguel, do you have a girlfriend back home?" Jemma asked when they had slowed to a walk on the final half mile to the barn.

"Sí."

"She's a beauty. He has pictures stuck all over the wall by his bunk. If I were younger, I'd give you a run for her." Bo's light teasing missed its mark.

Miguel stopped his horse and stared at Bo. "You no go for her. She promised to marry me."

"Don't worry, partner." Bo looked to Jemma for help.

Jemma nudged Brandy between the two other horses. "Any girl would pick you, Miguel, over this broken down wrangler. I think the world of him, but he has a lot of rough edges." Jemma winked at Bo. "It's too late for a senorita to break him in, but you, you're still young enough to learn how to make a girl happy." Jemma waited a beat.

"Sorry," Miguel said to Bo.

Jemma leaned over and hugged Brandy while the wranglers sorted out the little misunderstanding.

Bo nodded then headed his horse toward the barn. "I'm not so old that I don't remember being in love and being away from her. When will you see her again?"

"I have my papers and we are trying to get hers. I'm hoping to marry her in the spring."

Jemma stopped Brandy at the barn and dismounted. "Will you be leaving us then?"

"I hope not. We will find her a job and a little house to rent somewhere in the valley. By then, I should have enough saved. I save very hard."

They unsaddled the horses and Miguel brought her one of the pictures from the bunk house.

"What's her name?" She was young and pretty and stood before an old whitewashed church.

"Juanita. We lived in the same village in Mexico and went to school together. She is practicing her English. She will work hard. The only problem is immigration."

Jemma handed back the photo and Miguel touched the face in the picture.

"I'm sure everything will work out fine. It will be worth the wait." Jemma led Brandy into the stall and groomed her while mentally wrangling with desire, possession, jealousy, freedom, independence, respect – all the conflicting emotions a new relationship can be subject to.

It was after nine by the time Tucker managed to call Jemma. The day had been long and hectic but stimulating as lightning on a nearby tree. "Hey, C-Girl, how was today?" Tucker loved teasing her about being a cowgirl. She was probably as happy about the name as he was about the way she'd shortened "investigator." He took a sip of the camomile tea she'd given him last week to help him get to sleep. He wasn't sure he liked the taste or that he'd let it steep long enough.

"Good, Gator, what did you bite into today?"

"You first. Sorry I missed you before the interview. I haven't seen you since Sunday." He eased back into his lounge chair. Her voice soothed him much more than the bland tea did.

"Gator, I've missed you, too. We've got to figure out a way to see each other more often."

"You know how unpredictable my job is." Not to mention the long round-trip drive to and from the ranch.

"Mine's calmed down now that we're in the off season. It gives me more time to miss you. I rescued someone today, two someones."

Jemma smiled at him from a framed photo on the table next to his chair. "Oh? I hope you didn't put yourself in any danger."

Jemma told him about the cats. "He's Undercover Kitty. If I were to keep them – which I'm not – I should name the male after you, Detective Tucker."

"Great. A scaredy cat who hides. That's flattering. Then I'll name the girl after you, Jemma Kitty." Tucker recognized the warmth in her voice and knew she wouldn't give up the cats now. "How was the interview?" Tucker hoped his tone was light enough. Qualified, intelligent, energetic, there was no way she wouldn't get the job.

"It went well. My qualifications aren't exactly what she's looking for but I think the job would be easy enough. I'm not looking forward to working swing shifts."

"They stink, but people get used to it." If she was determined to become a detective, she had to start where there was an opening, since she didn't have a degree in law enforcement. Encouraging her was noble and admirable, he reminded himself while nodding at her photograph.

"I'd rather not talk about it and jinx the outcome. Besides, it's only a stepping stone to the real stuff. I can't wait until I can actually puzzle out the crimes, figure out the who and why, like you do. We couldn't be a team, of course, but we could still help each other. How long does it take for someone to work up to being an investigator?"

"Now, Jemma." Tucker refrained from telling her to "calm down." His cousin had clued him in on the adverse reaction women had to that phrase. "We've been through this. It takes years and years. It may not ever happen for you. There is no fast track." Tucker swallowed some tea, the events of the day gradually leaving his head. Work faded with the sound of her voice, with the rhythm of her words and the little intake of her breath. Truth be told, he didn't always listen to what she said as much as enjoyed the connection.

"I heard there was some excitement in Hickory Hills today."

"Let me guess. Bo." That man probably knew more than Tucker did about the fire, police, first responders, sheriff and who knows what else happened in the county. Especially now that he wasn't on trail rides every day.

"You know my sources too well. Come on, give."

"I can't do that. It's privileged information." This was a game they played many nights over the phone. Jemma tried to wiggle out the details of crime in Watauga County and Tucker stayed firm in his silence. So far, it was Tucker at ninety-eight, Jemma, zero.

"I'm practically working in the sheriff's department. I already know it was a break-in at the top of the mountain. From what the neighbor says, it couldn't have happened to a more appropriate lady."

Tucker roused from his languor. "What do you mean by that?" Don't let Jemma be involved in this.

"She's the Property Owners Association president and not popular with some of the owners in the development."

Tucker listened as Jemma told him about Ann's plans approval troubles and Karen's view of the situation. Then she relayed what she'd overheard in Perfect for Framing. When she asked him again for details, he sidetracked her by asking about her construction project. By the time they'd talked about Brandy, the newly christened DT and JK, he heard her yawn. He wished he was there.

"One more thing. What are you doing two Friday evenings from now?"

"What do you suggest?" A quiet evening at this house. They could eat in. He could buy something prepared at the grocery store since neither of them cooked.

"We've been invited to a party at Perfect for Framing for exhibitors, neighbors, guests and friends. It starts at eight."

"I'll say 'yes' but you know my schedule is subject to change."

"Elvis will be there."

"In that case, I'll make it a priority."

Chapter 5
THE WEEKEND, A WEEK LATER

WRANGLER BO HELPED Jemma unload the breakfast bar at Karen's home. A pang of loss of her beautiful creation hit her unexpectedly. She shrugged off the thought of her becoming possessive of anything. While Jemma bolted the end of the bar to the wall, Bo stabilized the other end.

"This is just like I envisioned." Karen flitted around testing the doors, opening and closing the drawers. "Honey, these drawers glide smooth as lipstick into its case."

Jemma nodded in acknowledgment and she and Bo returned to the truck. She'd spent the better part of last week building the top for the breakfast bar, loving every minute of the work. She had biscuit-joined four boards together, cut them to size, sanded, routed the edges, and lightly stained the oak before mitering the five skirt pieces, routing them to match the drawer fronts. With four coats of satin polyurethane on the top and base, the grain of the wood stood out. Reluctant to let it go, she bolted the top in place.

Karen popped her gum and cooed over the breakfast bar. "Thank you for working so fast to get this ready. I set up a card table in its place and pretended to use it. My husband couldn't understand my enthusiasm."

"It'll be next Saturday before I can bring the corner cabinet." Riding Brandy every day would have to wait. She'd built in some extra time into her woodworking schedule because of the winter weather. So far, she could hit the trail a few times next week.

Karen's phone rang. "Yes, she's here. I love the work she brought today." To Jemma, she said, "It's for you."

"Jemma? I'm Petula Windsor and live in Hickory Hills, at the top. I have a guest house that I'd like for you to do some carpentry work in. Since you're in the subdivision, would you stop by and take a look?"

Jemma looked at Karen, remembering her opinion of the lady. "Sure. We're finishing up here so we'll be up directly." She'd get to see the crime scene, even though it was probably cleaned up and back to normal. A break-in wasn't much, but it was as close as she could get to playing CSI.

Karen's eyebrows hit the top of her forehead. "You're going to Madam President's place?"

Jemma nodded. "Mind if I take some photos of the breakfast bar for my files?" Bo loaded the tools in the truck and swept up the sawdust around the base of the bar while Jemma snapped some shots.

"Honey, if you have a bill, I'll write you a check." Karen reached for her purse.

With Karen's check in her pocket and a sense of success thumping through her body, Jemma drove Bo to the top of the mountain to meet Madam President. How could she find out where the break-in happened without actually asking?

"Who needs a house that big?" Bo gawked as he parked the truck. "We could throw a mighty fine party in there. Everyone could sleep over. I bet you could sleep in a different bedroom for two weeks straight."

Petula met them at the walk to the guest house. Jemma expected a witch complete with broomstick from Karen's description of the problem-causing woman. Instead Jemma saw an aging woman, careful with her appearance. Bet she had English antiques in the main house. Her portrait would be taken standing next to the fireplace with the camera pointed up so Petula could have a commanding look to her.

"My guest house needs some changes and it's so hard to get someone to do these little things. You know what I mean?" Petula said as she led them into the house.

"Yes, I've heard that." Jemma, thwarted from seeing the house with the break-in, followed Petula, and Bo followed Jemma.

"I have two projects for you, both upstairs. I'll give you a quick tour down here first."

A stone fireplace dominated the living room which was open to the kitchen/dining area. The tongue and groove cathedral ceiling soared overhead; the hand hewn stair railing drew her attention.

She led them to the downstairs bedroom. "The view from the bed is spectacular this time of year." Petula turned to face the window.

"Wow!" Jemma looked past the glass door to the mountain tops. No curtains or blinds blocked the view out the glass door nor the two bookend windows. "I'll bet your guests hate to leave."

"It is beautiful. I never get tired of it."

Jemma turned. "It's also captured in the mirror. Great placement." Jemma picked up a painted fist-sized stone that adorned the vanity. The crude paint strokes hinted at two figures connected by fingers and swirling currents.

"My brother did that when we were kids." Petula reached her hand and Jemma gave her the stone. She carefully positioned it in its place in a custom fitted wood holder.

"This is so beautiful. May I take some pictures?" Her photo of snow tipped peaks of rows and rows of mountains clear into Tennessee could be an addition to her Perfect for Framing collection.

Petula didn't answer.

"It's a hobby of mine, but feel free to say 'no'." The mountains through the leafless trees would be perfectly framed by the doorway. The lighting was right.

"I'm flattered. I decorated the guest house myself. Take all the photos you want."

Jemma took photos then Petula led them back to the living room. An open loft had two areas divided by a bathroom. While they climbed the stairs opposite the fireplace, Jemma admired the beadboard cathedral ceiling.

"Here, under the eaves," Petula said. "I'd like to knock out these two short closets on either side of the dormer and put in drawers. The bottom ones will be deep, of course, and the top ones shallow. Do you think you can do that?"

"Yes, Mrs. Windsor. It won't be difficult. I'll make the two bottom ones four feet long, four feet deep and eight inches tall. The top ones will be only two feet deep. What is the other project?"

"Please call me Petula. I'm not that much older than you."

Jemma stared at her as she walked to the open loft area. She heard Bo whisper, "She's got a good twenty years on you, despite the work."

Jemma stifled a smile. "What work?" she whispered back.

"See the wrinkles around her ears? If she was a man, she'd be shaving face hair from behind her ears."

How did Bo know these things? They scrambled to catch up with Petula.

"This closet needs to be transformed into a storage area. Since this is my office, I need more storage space for papers and files. I want to do away with that cabinet."

A tall, tasteful cabinet stood in the corner. The maid missed dusting the top, but Jemma doubted Petula knew about it. She'd have to get a step stool to see that high, even with her three-inch heeled boots. "Do you want built-in file drawers?"

Petula nodded. "With locks. And a pull-out section to keep disks. I know some people consider them obsolete but I still use them. Oh, and a place for software boxes."

"I can make some sketches and email them to you." Jemma knew this would be simple for her CAD program.

"I like that idea. Come on over to my desk. Excuse the mess; I'll write down my address for you." Petula pranced as if on a runway, head held high.

While Bo measured the inside of the closet, Jemma followed Petula to the desk. An open jeweler's box sat next to the desk lamp, with a bracelet glittering inside. "That is gorgeous."

"Go ahead. Pick it up. I hold it up to the light every time I'm up here." Petula's eyes gleamed as bright as the stones in the bracelet.

Jemma held the bracelet so the light shown through it. Diamond after diamond, lined up like soldiers on parade. Jemma had never in her life held such an expensive piece of jewelry. "Someone loves you very much."

Petula licked her lips. "You could say that."

Jemma put it down, then couldn't help but notice a page with cutout words taped to it: ***Let her build. Back off – or else.*** She couldn't ask if it related to the break-in since she wasn't supposed to know anything about it.

"Here you go." Petula gave Jemma a slip of paper. "Oh, I see you noticed my threatening letter. It looks like it was cut out of some art magazine. See the snippets of artwork in the background? Feel the thickness of the paper." Petula huffed. "It was slipped under the door at the house yesterday. Someone was too cheap to send it through the mail."

"Did you contact the police?" Tucker should know about this.

"What for? My husband's study was broken into last week and they haven't solved that yet." Petula looked wide eyed at Jemma. "Say, aren't you related to the Chases that own the dude ranch outside of town? The one with the body in the woods? I read about it in the newspapers in the fall."

Jemma swallowed a groan. "Yes. Bo, are you finished with your measuring?"

"Was that the first dead body you've ever seen?"

"Yes. Why?" It was the only dead person she'd ever seen. She'd never even been to an open casket funeral.

"No reason. The only body I've ever seen was my first husband's. He was shot by an intruder. I had nightmares for months. It was a long time ago but that's why I was so upset at the break-in last week. Why, what if one of us had been home?"

If Jemma wouldn't be able to see the study where the actual crime had been committed; at least, she was on the same property. Bo handed her the tape measure and nodded, indicating that he had all the measurements.

"You're lucky that you weren't. You ought to tell the authorities about that letter." Tucker would hear about it during their nightly phone call.

"Maybe I will the next time they contact me. Do you think it's connected to the break-in?"

"The point is that it could be connected." Jemma did some figuring on a piece of paper and quoted Petula a price. When Petula hesitated, Jemma mentally reviewed the costs to see if she could reduce the price.

"I'll double the price if you can get this to me by Monday."

Jemma blinked, took a moment for her offer to register, then thought about shifting Karen's cabinets to later in the week.

"I know you are doing work for someone else but I do hate to wait. Once I make up my mind to do a project, I expect it to be done immediately."

Jemma had the impression that few people turned down a request from Petula. Jemma glanced at Bo, more to gather her wits than for answers. She may be a demanding little woman but she had influence. A good word from her would help. "They could be ready by Monday morning, weather permitting."

Bo took Jemma to Lowe's Hardware where she bought wood and hardware, then dropped her off at the Miller workshop where she built the drawers and face for the built-in dresser, cut the closet shelf and worked on the file drawers. Sanding took a little longer than she'd hoped but she managed to spray on one coat of polyurethane before Bo picked her up after his errands.

While helping Alma clean up after dinner, Jemma told her about the work to be done for Petula Windsor, including the incentive to be put first in line.

"Watch out for her," Alma said, draining the water from the sink. "Did you know Petula's land once belonged to Lottie's people? They lost it due to back taxes."

"That's happened to a lot of people here. They work hard, raise crops and children, but don't have money to spare." Jemma started the dishwasher.

Alma dried her hands and leaned against the counter, facing Jemma. "When her great-grandson Travis was ten, an old cabin on Petula's land caught fire. Petula used to sneak there and smoke cigarettes. That's one thing her husband won't put up with."

"Good for him." Smoking was such an old fashioned habit, not to mention disgusting.

"It was a cabin on the old homestead and Travis used to visit there. One time, she saw him and accused him of spying on her. The place caught fire shortly after that and she proclaimed to anyone and everyone that he started it. She produced Travis' baseball cap. He was found not guilty of arson due to lack of evidence, but he moved to his uncle's down in Hickory."

Jemma shook her head. "That's terrible." Around her Petula may have acted pretentious but not mean. Good manners and a pretty face could hide many sins.

"What's more, Petula recently approached Lottie to sell her more land. She wants to control the other side of the mountain." Alma wiped her hands and spread out the dish towel to dry.

"Will Lottie do that?" Maybe Petula was too self-absorbed, like they claim teens were these days. Jemma headed to the back door and Alma walked to the dining room door.

"She'll hang onto it with her last breath." Alma raised her voice to carry across the room. "She's having the papers drawn up to give it to Travis now so as when she's gone, it won't be a part of the will. Lottie loves that boy. Says he deserves to live there on account of what that woman did to him. All I'm saying is you be careful." Alma put her hand on the light switch.

"I won't cross her. I'll get this over with quickly." Tenderness filled Jemma. Her aunt would look after Jemma, even if she didn't need it.

"I hope she pays right away. Rich folks sometimes are the worst to pay." With that, Alma turned off the lights.

That evening after e-mailing the sketches to Petula, she received a quick approval. Thank the stars since she'd almost completed the project. Jemma and Tucker spent an hour on the phone. "I had to spend part of the check from Karen on a cat tree. DT and JK were scratching up my furniture. DT loves it, especially the treats I give him when he reaches the highest landing."

"Smart cat. He's training you well."

Jemma didn't care that she babbled on about the cats. They were so cute and the world needed to hear about it. "JK doesn't like the treats. I'm having to use the squirt bottle on her. I hate the way she panics when I yell 'no' and then squirt her with water."

"I take it you plan to keep the cats."

"I've fallen in love with them. It's too late to let them go." Jemma watched the black one pounce on the little girl at the foot of the bed.

"You won't believe what I investigated today. Someone set a portable toilet on fire."

Details? Without her prying it out of him. *Ti-ti-tat* her heart beat double time. "Why? Better yet, how?" Jemma tugged the blanket up to her chest and snuggled in bed with the phone between her head and the pillow. He seemed closer.

"We don't know the who or the why. We assume it was vandals. The how is by lighting either the soap dispenser which is sixty-one percent alcohol or the toilet contents."

"What did it look like?" Jemma adjusted the pillow to keep the phone closer to her ear. JK curled up near Jemma's feet. How long would DT leave his sister alone?

"A block of melted plastic with the toilet bowl in outline.

What about you? Did you get to ride Brandy today?"

"A short one. I took on another small construction project."
Lots of interesting work, new kitties and a wonderful man in her
life. Jemma's heart sent out a "thank you" to the universe.

"Tell me about this one."

"It's also in Hickory Hills, for Petula Windsor. She wants me
to build in some dressers and customize a closet for office storage." She waited for him to give details about the break-in but he
didn't. "I happened to see a threatening note on her desk."

"Repeat that part about the Windsor note."

Jemma repeated it, reveling in her role as clue collector. "Do
you think she wanted me to see it?"

"Why do you say that?"

"The whole desk experience felt staged. She knows that I know
you." Keep to the data, no need to embellish, she told herself.

"We haven't tried to keep it a secret. But our seeing each
other wouldn't be important to anyone else. More interesting is
why she didn't call it in."

"Her opinion of the sheriff's department isn't high at the
moment. You were supposed to find the thief immediately. Maybe she's saving the note to show at the POA meeting coming
up." Jemma paused. "I know. She's going to use it in her lawsuit
against the lady trying to build in the subdivision." The black
kitty sniffed JK and curled up next to her.

"Okay, C-Girl. I'll bite. What lawsuit?"

Jemma told him what little she knew. "Good thing the
break-in wasn't in the guest house. You should see the glittering
bracelet she keeps on the desk. Not that it was to my taste, but
it was beautiful."

"You don't wear much jewelry that I've seen."

"Give me something in a beautiful Saslow jewelers' box and
I'll wear it."

Tucker met Jemma after breakfast early Sunday morning. The vapor trails in the clear cold sky crisscrossed in a lopsided star pattern. He'd gotten into the habit of coming later since Alma wouldn't let him pay for his breakfast. Jemma introduced him to DT and JK before she went with him to the stables with a thermos of coffee and some leftover ham biscuits for a snack later. He couldn't help it, he took her in his arms and hugged her so long she started to squirm.

She mumbled against his neck. "At least let me put down the thermos."

He released her, letting his hands rest for a moment on her hips and simply smiled. His throat was dry, something that had been happening more and more often when he thought about her.

"Do you want to ride Visa today?" Jemma carried her saddle to Brandy and put it on.

Tucker did the same with Visa. "No riders again this week?" Visa's breath was white in the cool air he noticed as he checked the tightness of the saddle's cinch.

"More skiers. That's fine with me since I get to work on cabinets." Jemma mounted and clicked for Brandy to leave the barn. "No reflection on you, Brandy."

Tucker'd been riding with Jemma most Sunday mornings since they met in early fall. Today they'd ride to Raccoon Run and on up to the top of the mountain. He started off beside Jemma but as the trail narrowed, he dropped behind her. Brandy wasn't about to let another horse take the lead. Tucker settled in the saddle and enjoyed the view, both of the woods and of Jemma. She sat tall, hips swiveling with Brandy's gate. Her thick single braid almost touched the back of the saddle.

A squirrel chattered at them from high in a tree. Clouds gathered in the south, sign of a wet snow on the way. Calm had eased into Tucker by the time they reached the ridge an hour later and dismounted. They tied the horses to a tree in companionable silence before spreading a blanket on the brown grass.

Tucker admired the layers and layers of mountains to the east, mindful that they created their own weather systems with fog in one valley, sleet in the next and blue skies overhead.

Jemma poured him a cup of coffee as they sat side by side looking down on the valley. "How long until you figure out who did the break-in?"

Tucker sipped the coffee, ignoring the question. No way to predict something like that.

"Must have been something important in those files mentioned in the paper," she said, staring into the distance.

Somehow he'd come to like her nosiness about his business, not that he'd let her in on anything. "One of those biscuits would be tasty about now." She didn't seem to hear him.

"Ward Windsor's a decision maker at the bank. Could it be a client wanting to hide something?" Jemma snapped her fingers and looked at him. "I know. Someone's embezzling from the bank and he had proof he kept at home to be safe."

"Nope, but I do like the way your mind works." He bumped his shoulder against hers. She didn't react so he bumped her again. "Alma's outdone herself with these biscuits. Is there another one?"

Jemma flashed him a look of exasperation as she passed him the bag. "Something personal. Silly me, he'd keep bank files at work." She nibbled on her biscuit. "He was following Petula. No, he'd be too easy to spot and I doubt he could move very fast. I've got it. He was having her followed." She shifted and faced him.

Tucker quit chewing and narrowed his eyes, mentally replaying their conversations and checking to be sure he hadn't said anything specific about the case.

"He hired a private investigator. Local, probably looked in the phone book. Even a small town like Boone has to have one or two. I'm right, aren't I?"

Jemma's screwed-up smile was so smug there was only one thing to do. Tucker set down his cup and biscuit, took hers from her and set those down then growled and reached for her, pinning her to the blanket. "What makes you so smart? Hanging around with me?"

"Must be Alma's cooking."

He kissed her for a long time, hoping to replace her thoughts about his work with something better. It worked for a while.

As they mounted the horses for the ride back, Jemma said, "You can trust me with details, especially since no one was hurt in the break-in." She led them back down the mountain.

"It isn't a matter of trusting you." Tucker focused for a moment when Visa stumbled and recovered. Slick spots on the trail had developed from the ground thaw after the snow. "I know you won't tell anyone about the private investigator or the fact that he parked at the house above the Harmons and walked up."

"He did?"

Tucker groaned. The whole investigation played out in his head at the oddest times. Was it any wonder that he'd slip up once in a while?

Chapter 6

MONDAY

*J*EMMA LEFT BEFORE daylight and put two more coats of quick-drying polyurethane on the Windsor project. She packed the truck with a screw gun and other tools and the pre-cut wood pieces for installation as scheduled by Petula to begin at one.

Arriving a little early, Jemma loaded her arms with tools and approached the guest house. The door was open and she heard Petula shouting. "He's my boss! I can't not see him."

"He's your lover. You end it now if you want to remain my wife. Do you understand?" A man's deep voice barked.

Jemma put the tools down outside the door and returned to the truck for another load. She'd driven all this way and was not leaving until the job was done. That argument wouldn't last forever.

The voices had calmed by her third trip. Jemma peeked in the door this time and saw Petula rub her husband's arm. "Love, that private investigator caught me coming from the shower and Darryl getting ready to get in the shower. Naked doesn't mean sex."

He couldn't be that dumb, Jemma thought as she put down a load. She made several more trips to the truck before Mr.

Windsor left, edging his way around the tool and wood pile. He looked up, nodded brusquely, and strode to the main house. The anger in his eyes would make a good study. She'd light the eye area and leave the rest of his face in shadow. Either she had him well trained or he didn't care, thought Jemma. If that were the case, why stay with her? Habit, loneliness, maybe laziness. It was easy to see Petula's motivation – money and prestige.

"Come on in," Petula said. "Family discussion. You're single, aren't you?" Not waiting for an answer, she continued, "Sometimes husbands are more trouble than they're worth. Don't worry. I have him trained to wag his tail when I flash my eyes at him."

She's deluding herself, Jemma thought as she carried everything upstairs.

Petula followed her, took off her bracelet and put it in the box on her desk. "I made the mistake of wearing this around Ward. I'm not usually that careless. I had to explain who gave it to me."

Jemma wanted to ask but didn't and started on the office closet first. She'd already cut boards to length so it was just a matter of screwing the supports to the walls before installing the shelves. The slides for the drawers were easy to put in and the file drawers glided smoothly.

While Jemma worked, Petula called her brother and relayed the encounter with her husband. "Don't you turn against me, too," Petula said just before hanging up the phone. To Jemma, she said, "How long do you think this will take?"

"I'll be able to finish late this afternoon."

"Good. I should be home early today."

Jemma worked steadily and with deep concentration for the next few hours and was sweeping up the sawdust when Petula returned. Jemma gave her the bill.

Petula said, "I'll give this to Ward to pay. He'll have it ready tomorrow, if you want to come by around twelve-thirty."

Jemma nodded.

Petula followed her out the door. "Your work is well worth the money. The last job I had done, I was blind-sided by a dishonest man, a lay preacher, no less. One of those who uses God as a false front to lure the trusting into hiring him." Petula tugged on her blouse sleeves and stood tall. "I had to sue him for charging double what he estimated. He lied on the stand with one hand on the Bible and facing the judge. He said he prayed to God what to do and was told to proceed with charging me that outrageous amount partly because I could afford it."

"Did you win?"

Petula raised one eyebrow. "Of course I won. I always win."

On the way home, Jemma turned left at the New Market light and recognized the passenger in a van as it passed her on the four-lane highway. Flora stared straight ahead and didn't notice Jemma. The van turned onto old Hwy 421, Jemma's route, then turned into a subdivision. On impulse, Jemma followed them, playing detective. She drove past the driveway after they turned in. Jemma turned the truck around, parked in the next driveway and didn't have long to wait. Jemma laughed at herself for looking for strange behavior. This was not CSI but stalking, snooping at the least. Flora's husband was a real estate agent, for goodness sake. The sign in the yard advertised his agency and had "under contract" listed in bold letters.

Jemma grabbed her camera when she saw them carrying out an antique settee and put it in the back of their van. "Probably legitimate," she murmured as she photographed them carrying out two matching chairs, a side table and a painting. When they locked the house door, Jemma left, not wanting to be noticed.

Her heart pounded all the way down the mountain, both from the leftover rush and with the anticipatory excitement of the case. When she got home, she searched the real estate section of the newspaper. The house was listed as "fully furnished." The kitties followed her upstairs and fought over Jemma for attention while she downloaded the photos. All had remarkable details, especially of the faces of Flora and Darryl. After shutting down the computer, she carried each cat under an arm back downstairs and lectured them. Jealousy wasn't good in any shape or form.

Chapter 7
TUESDAY

*J*EMMA SPENT THE morning with the horses and wranglers. Brandy welcomed her with a series of head bobs. Even though the guests were skiers and no one wanted to ride this week, the hands took the horses for a short ride to keep them alert and give a little exercise. Jemma drove up the gravel winding road in Hickory Hills at twelve-forty, she didn't want to be early like yesterday. The Killdares, a group out of Texas, blasted Celtic rock from the CDs Jemma had bought at the Grandfather Scottish Games in July. The music brought back images of the young, fit and lean bagpiper, enticing in his kilt and heavy boots when he leaned back and fingered the pipe while squeezing the plaid bag with his arm. After his solo, he raised his left arm and his biceps flexed as he pumped his fist in the air in time to the beat.

Jemma finger-waved to a car on the first curve, then repeated the wave a few seconds later to another car. She slowed at the curve with the rhododendron slick, admired the deep green leaves curled under to protect them from the freezing temperature, then saw yet a third vehicle and reduced the volume on the CD. The driver looked like Ann from the gallery.

Jemma had no idea traffic was this busy during the lunch hour. As she drove the circular driveway at the top of the mountain, she saw smoke and imagined a warm fire would feel good on a day like this. Two vehicles were in the garage. She rang the doorbell and listened to Ward's steady tread from the left side of the house. His face was more ordinary than the last glimpse she'd had of him. She didn't want to photograph him now. "Come in. I'll go get my checkbook."

Jemma waited inside, admiring the ornate stair rail off to the side. A faint odor of smoke hung in the air. The corners of the eight-inch crown molding were mitered just right. The six- inch baseboard balanced the room. The stone work on the fireplace went from floor to the top of the cathedral ceiling. An ornately framed painting of Petula hung over the mantle above the fire-place. No fire.

Ward returned and handed Jemma a check. "Petula is well satisfied with your work. I appreciate that you worked quickly. You don't know how rare that is in the construction industry. I'll be happy to refer people to you."

Jemma thanked him, appreciating the referral almost as much as the payment. She stuck the check in her jeans pocket, then asked, "Are you burning brush out back?"

"No. Why?"

"I thought I saw smoke." Jemma looked at Ward expectantly.

"Petula's around here somewhere." He called up the stairs and waited to hear her respond.

They looked at each other then rushed out the door. Jemma rounded the house and yelled back to Ward. "Call nine-one-one. It's the guest house."

Jemma bolted in through the open guest house door. She ducked down to get below the smoke and realized that the fire was on the back porch. "Anyone here?" she yelled, coughing. She grabbed the fire extinguisher from the kitchen wall and tried to open the back door. No luck.

The key was missing from the dead bolt but she rattled the

door anyway. Flames shot from down the far end of the back porch. She yelped and headed down the hall to the bedroom. If her recollection was correct, there was a door off the bedroom leading to the porch. She'd photographed the view using the door as a frame. Strange to waste a thought on that now.

Smoke was heavy but she didn't see actual flames in the hall. Dropping to her knees, she hugged the extinguisher close as she crawled. Elbows and knees banged the wood floors for what seemed like an hour. When she made it to the bedroom door, she let go of the fire extinguisher, seeing something more important.

Petula lay on her back in the doorway. Her face, pale, waxy and gray, caused Jemma to hesitate. Jemma grabbed her by the shoulders and dragged her down the hall, to the front door and onto the porch. The body was heavy but Jemma summoned her strength to make it to the open air. Jemma had to control her coughing before she could concentrate on Petula, then shook her and called her name.

"Oh, God, help me now," Jemma said, as she checked for Petula's pulse. The smell of wet ash and the sizzle of water on fire alerted Jemma that Ward had hooked up a hose around back and sprayed the flames.

No pulse. Jemma straddled Petula and began percussions. "One and two and three and four" she said to pace herself, hoping against her intuition that she'd be successful. A car drove up and she heard a woman say, "Lucky, you take the fire and I'll help out here." As footsteps approached, she did not pause in her counting and pressing on Petula's chest. She heard a chest bone crack but kept working.

"I'm Maggie, a First Responder. Do you want me to take over?"

Jemma nodded but kept working until Maggie was in position before handing over the rhythm. The sound of far-off sirens registered when Jemma stepped back and watched Petula's face intently, hoping for a gasp, a cough, anything to show she was still alive. "Come on, come on," she urged under her breath.

"Any minute now ..."

Heavily booted feet pounded the front porch. Someone led her off the porch and threw a blanket over her. She had to cough some more before accepting water to drink. Someone relieved Maggie who joined Jemma in watching and waiting. She heard the EMT command "clear" before they used the defibrillator on Petula. They administered the shock series three times.

"She's gone," Maggie whispered, then turned to Jemma. "I'm sorry."

"Me, too. I only met her a few days ago but it's a shock for this to happen to anyone." Jemma looked at Maggie for the first time. "Do I know you?"

"We met at Tucker's birthday party a few months ago. I'm one of his cousins. Lucky's around back with the fire."

Jemma watched the EMT still working with Petula on the porch, then saw Ward come around to the front of the guest house. He smiled at her in the yard. "I think we caught it in time. Thank God you saw that smoke."

His satisfied grin filled Jemma's heart with horror.

"Much longer, and the guest house, maybe even the main house would have been goners. I have a lot to thank you for."

Jemma opened her mouth but no words came out. Time stretched and every inevitable moment played out in slow motion. She pointed to the porch. Ward's smile faded as he took in the scene. "No!" He lurched to the EMT. "Is she? Is she?" A fire fighter pulled him back.

Detectives Tucker and Graves arrived shortly after the fire truck and emergency vehicles. Graves went around back. Tucker sucked in his breath when he saw Jemma leaning against the EMT vehicle. "You all right?" he called over to her. After her nod, he asked Maggie, "What are you doing on this side of the county? Not enough to do over by Sugar Mountain?" He tried to assess the situation but caught himself looking at Jemma every few seconds.

"Lucky and I came to Meat Camp for a quilt. He wants one for his wife for Christmas."

"He's here? Between the two of you, this incident looks under control."

"Jemma's the one who pulled her out." Maggie looked at each of them then mumbled something about being needed elsewhere.

Jemma shrugged out of the blanket and moved around to the side of the vehicle. "I'm okay, but she isn't."

Jemma's eyes were twice their normal size in her pale face. Tucker watched as the EMT disconnected the defib unit and signaled for the gurney. The EMT shook his head at Tucker to indicate that the victim hadn't made it. Tucker went to Jemma and grasped both her arms. "Do you want to tell me about it now or later?" Smoke hovered over her hair, dark smudges marred her face, but she looked unharmed. If something had happened to her ... a part of him wanted to yell at her not to take chances and another part was simply grateful that she was well and her gutsy self had tried to be a hero.

Her eyes filled with tears and he pulled her into his arms. "Go ahead and cry," he whispered. She shook and he held her tighter, wishing he could take her home and be with her to help her body and mind adjust to the reality of unexpected death, of trying hard to save someone and failing. He knew the feelings well.

Jemma pulled away and wiped her face. "I might as well tell it now." She gave a straightforward account without much emotion except for a shudder at the end.

She must be mistaken. She had to have turned Petula over. "You say she was face up and you dragged her out on the deck. Did she say anything?"

Jemma shook her head. "I think she was already dead. She must have inhaled a lot of smoke. I know it was hard to see." Jemma swallowed hard. "That back porch has a roof over it. The smoke funneled into the bedroom."

Tucker visualized her movements, almost felt the smoke burn his eyes. She must have dragged Petula fifty feet. An unconscious person weighed twice as much, or so it seemed. "The bedroom outside door must have been open. I need to check on things. Will you be okay?" He squeezed her arm, eager for contact but mindful of his duties.

"Sure. Go."

"You ought to go to the hospital in the ambulance and be checked out." Shock could set in, he thought but didn't want to inadvertently plant the idea.

"With a dead person? I'm fine, honest. I'm not going to any hospital."

"Do you want me to have someone drive you home?" He'd do it himself if he could.

"No. I'll rest here a while, then drive myself. You go, get to work." She pushed him away and folded the blanket.

Tucker hesitated, then went over to the Fire Marshall. "Accident?"

"Maybe the death was, but the fire was set."

"I thought I smelled a little petrol in the air." Tucker glanced at Jemma then walked around the house alongside the Fire Marshall. The soft ground squashed beneath his feet. Footprints would have been obliterated with all the pumped water and the firefighter tracks.

"It started on the left corner of the back porch. See the burn pattern? The V pattern shows hot at the bottom and expanded upward." He pointed to the sodden and charred remains. "It was confined to the porch, not much damage to the house itself. The accelerant was probably only used on the porch. Lucky your friend saw the smoke."

"Why was the smoke so thick?" Tucker looked at the blackened porch soffit and the walls of the house.

"The wind is gusting today. With this being the top of the mountain and no trees on this side for thirty feet, I'd say nature helped it along. That and the oily rags used to set the fire."

Tucker checked out the view. It was long range, into Tennessee, he reckoned. Come summer, the trees over the crest would leaf out and block the view. "Okay if I go in the house?"

"The structure didn't suffer damage. You know the rules."

"Thanks." Tucker walked to the woods and turned to look at the fire damage from a distance. Instead, he saw something caught in a tree root. At his foot were two chewing gum wrappers. He made a trip to the car and returned to the spot to photograph and collect the wrappers. They didn't look weather worn.

Tucker walked back to the front of the house in time to see the medical examiner give the okay to load Petula into the vehicle. He stopped them, took a moment to look her over. He checked her pockets. Nothing. She'd seemed like a nice but distraught lady when he'd investigated the break-in. Pretty, too, even with the soot on her face. Close up, her face looked kinda weird. No defense wounds on her hands and fingers. The nail polish wasn't chipped. Maybe she tripped and fell. He let the EMTs take her away. He'd make sure he was available for the autopsy. Jemma waved as she drove away. He watched the truck as long as possible.

Once inside, he saw little smoke damage in the living room and kitchen. The hall ceiling was black, as well as the bedroom ceiling. Jemma's drag marks remained despite the rescue traffic. The exterior doorjamb was charred but everything else would clean up. Even the floors didn't have much water on them. Jemma had said she found Petula in the interior doorway, face up. Tucker searched the floor and around the back side of the door, then returned to the back door. There, on a side table between the doors, he found a long fireplace lighter. He made a mental note to ask whose prints of the SBI team.

Jemma headed home, hands firmly on the steering wheel and eyes fixed rigidly ahead. She was in control. Much as she'd planned on working on cabinets for Karen, she needed to clean up and settle down. Before she made it far down the road, Karen flagged her down.

"What's happening up there? Are you hurt? Come on in and have some tea, better yet, something stronger."

Jemma turned on the truck flashers since she was stopped in the road. "I need to get home and clean up." Jemma hadn't noticed until then the soot on her jacket and the back of her hands. "The Windsor's guest house caught on fire. Luckily, it was caught in time."

"Was anybody hurt? I saw Ward, then Petula go up earlier, while I was fixing lunch."

Jemma was about to answer when she changed tack. "What time was that?"

"A few minutes after twelve."

"Did you see anyone else go up the road?" There were only three houses further up from Karen's.

Karen shook her head. "Lots of days I see that brother of hers. He drives different cars from the dealership. At least, I assume it's him. I don't always glimpse the face. The only reason I notice is because it's lunch time and I'm in the kitchen. I'm not spying on them or anything."

"Did you see a vehicle parked up at your neighbors?" Tired though she was, she'd take a clue when it presented itself.

"No, two are vacant in the winter." Karen paused but Jemma didn't say anything. "After that, I sat down to lunch and didn't notice. I had the news on the TV so I wouldn't have heard anyone drive by. I didn't even know you were up there. Why? What's happened?"

Jemma hesitated. "Petula was caught in the fire. She didn't make it."

Eagerness faded from Karen's face. "Honey, I didn't expect that. I mean, I wanted to know what happened but I never in this world thought I'd hear that she was dead."

"Keep it to yourself. They have to contact the rest of her family." Jemma thought of Tucker and wondered if she'd said too much.

Karen's face was pale and her voice weak. "Besides Ward,

there's only her brother that I know of. What caused the fire?"

Jemma sighed. The adrenalin had drained out and she was tired. "I don't know. Let me hear if you find out anything, you living here and all. I need to get home and take a shower."

"I understand. I'll call you if I hear anything." Karen stepped back from the truck. "I can see the headlines now, 'DOA of a POA'."

Jemma groaned. "Cute, but tacky," she said as she waved goodby.

DETECTIVES TUCKER AND GRAVES sat in Ward Windsor's living room and waited for him to finish washing. He'd changed out of the suit and tie and into slacks and a dress shirt. When he returned, Graves expressed his sympathy then asked, "Would you mind telling us about what happened here?"

"My wife asked me to come home for lunch today; I usually eat in town. When I arrived, we had some soup and a sandwich. She asked me to write a check for the work done on the guest house. I went to my study and didn't see her after that." He motioned for them to sit and he did likewise.

"How long were you in the study?" Graves asked.

To Tucker, the man appeared composed, probably due to years of testing in the banking world.

"Twenty, thirty minutes. I decided to catch up on some reading while I was here."

"Did you hear anything unusual? See anyone?"

"Jemma Chase, the carpenter, came around a quarter to one and rang the doorbell. Other than that, I wasn't disturbed. This house was well built so sounds don't carry far."

"Has your wife been under stress lately?"

"She was upset about the break-in last week " Ward paused, then asked, "Did you know that her first husband was killed by an intruder? They never caught the man."

Graves scribbled a note on his pad. "What about the

information from the private investigator?"

Ward stood and walked to the fireplace. "We were working things out. She said that the affair with her boss was over. It hadn't lasted long." He didn't look at the detectives.

"Did you believe her?" Tucker noted Ward's increase in agitation.

"What difference does that make now?" He stared up at Petula's portrait.

"The fire was set." Tucker catalogued Ward's every move, every nuance in pitch change.

"I wondered about that. The fire was concentrated in the one corner of the porch."

"We're trying to establish your wife's state of mind. Had she been acting, well, erratically?" The husband was calm for the most part, not distraught like he'd be if it were Jemma. He shouldn't have let her skip the hospital or drive home alone.

Ward picked up one of the three brass globes displayed on the mantel. "She's always been passionate about things. This Property Owners Association has kept her excited." He stared at the globe in his hand, then hastily put it down. "You don't think she set the fire herself, do you?"

"Do you?"

"That's insane." Ward walked across the room to the front door. "She'd be crazy to set her own place on fire."

"Exactly."

"This is outrageous. My wife just died." His deep voice boomed off the cathedral ceiling. Finally, some emotion.

Tucker rose to his feet. "I know this is difficult, but the sooner we get this out of the way the faster we'll be able to find out who started the fire."

"It wasn't Petula and it wasn't me, in case I'm on your list. I was at the other end of this house, for pity's sake." Ward pointed with his whole arm for emphasis.

Graves stood beside Tucker and said, "We'd like permission to look through the guest house and her rooms in this house. It'd be faster if we did that now."

"Don't you need a search warrant or something like that?"

"We could do that, but your permission is good enough."

"I have nothing to hide. Go ahead and search. I'll be in my study."

ALTHOUGH IT WAS ONLY late afternoon, Jemma could barely hold her head up by the time she drove through the upright posts at Blue Falls Ranch and down the gravel lane. All she thought about was her shower in her cabin behind the lodge until Aunt Alma flagged her down from the porch. Alma wore her workout clothes, including a headband. Jemma parked, then willed her legs to carry her up the dozen steps to the front door.

"Come on in, child. You need to get out of those clothes." Alma fussed around Jemma and helped remove her ski jacket.

Jemma stumbled into the reception area and plopped into one of the huge leather chairs. "What? How did you know?"

"Your Detective Tucker called to see if you'd made it home safely. I'd just hung up the phone when I heard your truck coming down the drive." Alma unlaced Jemma's work boots and stripped off her socks.

"Sorry about interrupting your exercise," Jemma mumbled, her eyes closing. Alma had been exercising regularly since Randy came into her life. Jemma opened her eyes and realized the exercise clothes were new.

"Belly dancing can wait. I can un-pause that DVD anytime."

"I don't know why I'm so tired. I didn't do much."

"Your body sure did. I'll get you some tea to revive you enough to make it up to my room."

Jemma relaxed into the chair, images but not words firing in her brain. Flames on the porch, smoke in the hall, her own arms pushing down on a chest, her crying into Tucker's shirt. She heard crackling fire, sirens, the crack of Petula's rib, Tucker's reassurances. She dozed, then felt herself led upstairs, undressed, then put in a shower of warm water. Alma stayed in the bathroom and asked enough questions to keep Jemma awake. It worked. She dressed in the fresh jeans and a flannel shirt that Alma had retrieved from Jemma's cabin.

"I'm gonna call Lottie and let her know what's happened, so she'll know why you aren't working there this afternoon," Alma said before she left.

Revived, Jemma carried her smoke-filled clothes to the washer and started a load. Alma was still on the phone when Jemma entered the kitchen.

"Here, you talk to her," Alma said, handing Jemma the phone.

"Alma says you tried to rescue Petula," Lottie said.

"I was too late. The smoke got to her first." A vision of Petula's perfect face floated in Jemma's mind. Only the soot marred the image – that, and she no longer breathed.

"Couldn't have happened to a more deserving person. Alma said she told you what she did to my Travis. No cause for that. I don't wish anyone dead, but life may get easier around these parts with her gone."

"What do you mean?"

"She's been pestering me to chop down the old trees at the top of my side of the mountain. Said they was too close to her guest house. If she hadn't built so close to the line, they wouldn't be too close. Real reason was so she could claim a view. Only a fool would build on a windy ridge. Bet she had to drill a thousand-foot well to reach water. Served her right."

"She treated me okay and even paid on time." Jemma didn't know where the impulse to protect Petula's memory came from. She had been human for a while and now was gone. Like herself, she had plans involving tomorrow, next week, next year. Her actions had caused consequences. What had she done to deserve her life to go up with the smoke?

"Bet you was paid by her husband. He had to have the patience of a saint to live with that woman."

Jemma didn't know what to say.

"Glad to hear you didn't come to any harm. Will you be here tomorrow?"

"I'll be there in the morning." Using her hands to build something would help.

Jemma went to transfer her clothes to the drier then gulped. She pulled out the wet jeans and felt in the pocket. A soggy mass of paper was all that was left of the check given her by Ward Windsor.

Chapter 8

*W*HILE GRAVES SEARCHED the main house, Tucker centered his attention on the guest house loft office. Minor water damage had concentrated in the downstairs bedroom so everything upstairs was dry. After gloving his hands, the first thing he saw on her highly organized desk was the cut-out threat note. A set of loosely rolled house plans lay on a chair. He wished the SBI team would hurry up. The saved messages light was lit on the answering machine. He pushed the button and immediately recognized the voice as that of her husband. "I can't stand this any longer. If you won't end it, I will." Tucker loved answering machine messages, cell phone memories and e-mail, all trails to follow.

The front door opened. Tucker leaned over the loft railing. "What took you so long?"

"Cars and trucks parked every which way, blocking this road."

Happened every time, he thought. "There's a message on an answering machine up here, a computer and papers on the desk you'll need to bag."

"Fire Marshall called it arson," the photographer said as he came up the stairs.

"We don't know yet if the victim started it or someone else." Tucker retreated to the stairs during the photograph session.

"We'll take it from here. You're looking for motive. We're looking for evidence."

After the photographer had finished, Tucker looked through the Jemma-redesigned closet, noticing the fine craftsmanship. No rough edges, smooth sliding drawers. Mostly, the shelves were filled with office supplies. One locked file drawer was labeled "POA" and the other "Personal." At least, they were locked at one time. Pry marks around the lock of the closed drawers drew his attention. With his pen, he opened the drawers. Neatly labeled file folders were arranged in alphabetical order. The names belonged to POA members, he'd bet. "Take the files in the closet, too," Tucker said to the second SBI team member.

Tucker went over and picked up the house drawings on the chair. Penciled in was "Ann Dixon" and her address and phone number. Tucker jotted it down in his notebook.

A search around the rest of the upstairs and the kitchen and living area downstairs took a while but nothing interesting revealed itself. Champagne and beer were in the refrigerator. A photo of a young Petula and her brother sat on the mantel in the living room. Two toothbrushes in the bathroom were the only personal items there. They'd be bagged for evidence. Everything was looked at during a death by fire investigation. When he opened the bedroom closet door, two bathrobes hung amongst empty wooden hangers. Except for the office, the house was ready for guests. How long would it be until the smoke smell left this place? Commercial clean up crews would make short work here. They'd have to scrub the ceilings and upper walls, replace the back bedroom door and frame, probably replace the back window frames, too. What little water there was on the floor had already dried.

The path between the outside and inside bedroom doors had an area rug. Why did she fall? Did she trip? If it was just smoke, she could have crawled out. Why come in here in the first place if she set the fire herself? Tucker walked slowly from the porch, past the dresser and to the doorway where Jemma had found the body acting out scenarios. Her hands were empty so it wasn't to save something. If someone else set the fire, she would have had time to run out the front since Jemma said the front door was open. That could have pulled in the smoke. Did she see someone? Did someone chase her?

Graves joined him in the guest-house bedroom. "Nothing in the house, except a box of photos from her childhood. All of the pictures were of her and her brother. None of her parents."

"Any of her husband?"

"Not that I could find. Maybe she wasn't into photos."

"That's all we can do here. You said the fire was started with oily rags. What kind of rags?"

"Red shop towels. The kind you see at car dealerships, automotive repair shops."

"Why don't we pay another visit to the Ford dealership tomorrow? I'd like to see what was in those files first."

When Tucker called again, Alma answered the phone and invited him down to the ranch for supper. He showed up at six and Jemma motioned him over to a seat beside her. The round ranch tables were only partially full. Eight skiers sat at one table. The help and locals took up two more. Jemma had told him December was a breather season for the help since the fall leaf-looker crowd was past and the snows of winter were still ahead. This time of year the ski slopes relied on making snow.

"Hello, Randy," Tucker said as he sat and put his napkin on his lap. At least Randy wasn't a suspect this time.

"Hear you have another one." Randy buttered a slice of Alma's home baked bread.

Tucker looked at Jemma. "Not me," she said.

"Word spreads here faster than kudzu." Alma finished loading all the food on the three tables so as everyone could serve themselves family style before sitting next to Randy. "If it hadn't been for Jemma's horse Brandy," Alma said, addressing the skiers, "I never would have met Randy and Jemma'd never met her detective."

Tucker gulped at "her detective."

Randy added, "We'd never had stopped the dog poisonings. We'd like to help, like we did last time."

It'd been a while since Tucker had made it down to the ranch for supper but he quickly figured out that Alma and Randy were keeping time together. Smart idea, Tucker thought. Alma was a fine lady and a great cook. Convenient, too; she lived at the ranch right across the road from Randy. "You know I can't talk about the case."

"Mind if we do?" Alma asked.

"Couldn't stop you if I tried." Tucker lifted a piece of pot roast onto his plate and passed the serving plate to Jemma. When she took it from his hand, he mouthed, "You okay?"

She nodded but said nothing.

"It was a good turn of fate that Jemma came around that house when she did or the whole place would have burnt to the ground. Maybe the whole mountain top, the way I heard the wind was whipping," Alma said.

"If she hadn't had to make an extra trip to pick up the check, no telling what would have happened." Bo plopped some potatoes on his plate and passed the bowl to Miguel.

"Sounds like ya'll know more about this than I do." Tucker glanced around the table.

"Alma plied Jemma with questions while she took a shower. Maybe she said a little more than she ought," Randy said.

"Yeah. She was asleep on her feet, the way I heard it," Bo added.

"If Petula hadn't made her come back at that precise time ..." Alma didn't finish the sentence.

Tucker's eyes cut to Jemma for confirmation.

Jemma spoke up. "Can we talk about something else? I haven't had a chance to make a formal statement."

"Sure, Jemma," Alma said, then called over to the skiers,

"Let me know if you need more of anything. I figured you'd be hungry after a day skiing at Sugar Mountain. Did any of ya'll go on the tubing run or go ice skating?"

"Are you kidding? I'm a snow boarder and spend all my time on the slopes," a young man in baggy pants said.

The young woman next to him added, "Excuse his manners. Boarders have an image to live down to."

People concentrated on eating and the silence grew.

Tucker asked, "What's happening with you, Randy?"

"Same old, same old."

"How about you, Alma?"

"Tried a new recipe for desert, Better than Sex Yellow Cake from Jane Wilson's cookbook."

"I'll save some room."

More quiet except for forks and knives scraping plates.

Jemma looked at her friends and family around the table, then sighed. "Oh, go ahead. Talk about me as if I wasn't here."

A couple of people tried to talk at once. Alma got the upper hand. "My friend Lottie Miller, who lives across the mountain from the fire, heard that Petula tried to make it look like arson, then got caught in her own fire."

"I heard they had to hose down the little house, the woods and the big house. The whole development was scared. Everyone was in their yards with garden hoses trying to wet down their roofs," Bo said. "Glad it wasn't earlier when we had that snow. The water hoses would have been frozen."

"When's the funeral? I might go to that one just to see who shows up," neighbor Lyle Bishop said.

"You don't even know her," his wife Pearle said.

"I met her husband a time or two." Lyle got up and headed to the desert table.

The speculation continued into dessert. "She sure was a looker," Bo followed Lyle and took two pieces of pie. "She was polite to me."

Alma snorted. "She had more work done than Dolly Parton."

"What's wrong with that?" a skier asked, lining up behind Bo. "Dolly's running stronger than any old lady I know."

"Surgery's cheating," Clinton Triplett, a local, said.

Tucker liked the big man with a soft spot for little dogs and his late mamma. He could be found tending the dumpster station four days a week and could be counted on for the inside story when Tucker needed it.

"That's so last century," another skier said. "The eighties was about making money. The nineties about body art like tattoos and piercings. This century's about body sculpting as in sports, sustenance and surgery. I'll bet someone in here dyes her hair."

"That's different. They ain't cuttin' on their body," Alma said.

"You have pierced ears," the skier said, returning to his seat.

"He has a point there," Clinton said.

"Pierced tongue." The skier stuck out his tongue and displayed a gold ball.

"Oh, gross," Alma said, surprising Tucker with her slang.

The skier grinned and opened his shirt. "Tattoos? I know a great artist in Charlotte if you're interested."

"That's so nineties," Jemma said.

"And forties. I've got a tattoo on my shoulder," ninety-year-old Lyle added. "Want to see? I got it when I was with the army's mounted engineers in Panama in '36. Or was it in Germany during World War II?"

Pearle shook her head. "They believe you, Dear. Finish your pie."

Tucker helped Alma and Jemma clear the tables then followed Jemma out back to her cabin. She unlocked the door, reassuring Tucker that she'd learned her lesson about home safety.

Once inside, he wrapped his arms around her. "Hey, C-Girl, how are you holding up?"

"Good enough. I was shaky this afternoon, though. Do you get this way after you've dealt with a tough situation?" She looked into his eyes.

"Sometimes. You have to remember that I've been at this

for fifteen years or so." He kissed her with all the tenderness and understanding possible in one kiss. "Where are the kitties?"

"They'll be out soon."

She led him to the sofa where they sat and propped up their feet on the coffee table. "You're saying that I'll get used to it. If I get the job, I mean."

Tucker's gut tightened and he made an effort to relax. "If you get the job, you will be in communications and won't be dealing with anyone in person. You'll still get a rush from some of the desperate calls." He slid his arm around her shoulder and pulled her near. "You know it's not like CSI on TV. That's so unrealistic."

"Of course it is. Remember Star Trek? All that science fiction technology like communicators and bloodless operations? Some science lovers became inspired by the show and now we have cell phones and worm holes are a part of American slang."

"You're saying that soon I'll have iris scans to replace the finger printing system we set up only last year?" He couldn't help the scoffing tone to his voice.

"Not next week but within the decade. Not only that, DNA testing will be a handheld device, just you wait."

"In your opinion, CSI is to forensics what Star Trek is to current technology."

"Right. Gill Grisham and Captain Kirk. Hold on for the ride. In the meantime, I could work up to being an investigator like you."

Her breath tickled his cheek. "You could, but it will take years, maybe even a decade or so. It depends on openings, how you handle yourself." Her lips were inches away.

"Politics?"

"A little. I tend to keep out of that as much as possible. You know, how you handle this situation will be taken into account. Once you give your statement, you need to stay out of sheriff business. It may make a difference in you getting hired."

Jemma sat up straight. "Really? I hadn't thought of that. Do you want my statement now?" She stood up as his arm dropped to the empty seat. She went over to her computer and turned it on.

Tucker remained seated, bemused. She hadn't even checked for his answer. "Why don't you write it and I'll wait right here?" He slumped down and leaned his head on the back of the sofa.

"Don't you want to ask me some questions?" Jemma positioned her fingers above the keyboard.

"Put everything down, even if it seems irrelevant. Like why you were there at that particular time." While her fingers clicked away, Tucker spotted DT slinking low, stalking Tucker's jacket sleeve slung over a chair. DT clawed it and pulled the whole garment down on top of him.

Jemma yelled "no" and grabbed the garment away from the black kitty. "Did he do this?" she asked, pointing to a hole in the jacket lining.

"No. That's where my gun rubs. I've been meaning to patch it."

"I could iron on a patch for you. Or Alma could sew in a leather one. She's got this sturdy old sewing machine she uses for repairing all kinds of stuff."

"Iron-on patches. I've never heard of such a thing."

Jemma went to the hall and dropped down an ironing board from a hidden panel and plugged in a small iron. "I use these all the time on my work clothes. They don't look the best but who sees the inside of your jacket? At least I have the right color for the lining."

Tucker rested on the sofa and watched while Jemma cut a two inch square out of the patch material and ironed it over the lining hole, unplugged the iron and propped it up on the kitchen counter to cool. DT jumped on the ironing board in the hall and sniffed every inch. "He checks out everything I do," Jemma said while handing Tucker the repaired jacket.

"Thanks for doing this." Tucker lay the jacket aside and pulled Jemma to his side on the sofa.

"I didn't finished my statement."

"We have time for that later."

Chapter 9
WEDNESDAY

EMMA CALLED WARD WINDSOR early on Wednesday and confessed that she'd washed his check. They arranged for her to pick up another one that evening after five. Jemma was at Perfect for Framing when it opened at ten o'clock. "Hello Ann. I thought I'd take a look at where you put my photos on display." The intense images from yesterday's fire receded now that she'd rested.

"Come on up. I'll show you." Ann led the way to the loft and a three-foot-wide space holding six of the photos hung on the wall along with a photo of Jemma on horseback.

"Great arrangement." Astonishment and pride in her own work made Jemma grin. The frames enhanced the photos; Ann had good decorating sense.

"They should get some attention here. Christmas shoppers have been coming in regularly this week. Maybe you'll have your first sale soon. This black and silver frame sets off the icicles, don't you think?"

"Uh huh. And the dark wood pulls out the chocolate in the turkey's feathers." Her own signature almost glowed from the corner of the photograph. Jemma followed Ann back downstairs. "Did you hear about the excitement in Hickory Hills yesterday?"

Ann hesitated, then took a cloth and wiped down the front counter. "Yes, I heard." She concentrated on a spot.

Jemma debated with herself for a moment. "It happened about the time you left."

Ann straightened to her full five feet seven inches. "What do you mean? I wasn't out there yesterday."

Jemma looked down at her. Keep it light, she reminded herself. "Oh. I thought I waved at your car while I was driving up the mountain."

"You're mistaken. I was here all day yesterday. If you don't mind, I need to get to work."

"Right. I have to get going, too. See you."

Jemma could have sworn she'd seen Ann Dixon on Tuesday. She walked around to the alley behind the store and saw the dark blue Mustang GT convertible. Maybe it was another car just like this one; fat chance, in Watauga County. She returned to her truck and stopped in at the tax office at the court house. It was simple enough to find out the name and address of the sellers of the house she'd seen the Johnsons at on Monday. Tucker would call it meddlin' but she called it following the clues.

She left downtown, turned left at New Market Center onto Hwy 194. Todd General Store was a dozen miles down the winding road which loosely followed Elk Creek, the same Elk Creek that ran down Triplett Valley. The creek's headwaters were not too far above Todd. The only delay was when the narrow road was blocked by two trucks headed in opposite directions stopped while the two drivers talked. One tooted his horn in apology when he drove off.

Jemma parked in the gravel area on the other side of Todd General Store, across from the glade which held a small stage for music concerts on Saturdays in the summer.

Proprietor Bob Mann opened the old screen door for her. "Good to see ya. Alma called in the order. Gini is boxing it up as we speak." He closed the old wood door behind her, keeping in the heat from the pot-bellied stove. Padded stools were gathered around tables used in the summer for Tuesday night storytellers and on Fridays for bluegrass music jams. Jemma preferred her bluegrass in short bits, just like rap. The rhythms repeated too often for her liking.

Jemma went back to the preserves section but stopped to look at one of the many birdhouses for sale. She picked up one of the simple ones to see how it was constructed. She could do that, she thought, putting it back on the shelf before joining Gini. "Alma loves those pickled okra and that blackeyed pea dip. The ranch guests gobble them up during the afternoon coffee break."

"Be sure and get enough to carry you through the winter. We're heading for Florida after New Year's and won't be back until May." Gini grabbed a *Watauga Democrat* newspaper and began wrapping jars of sweet potato butter.

"May I see that?" Jemma asked, noticing the headlines, "DOA of the POA," Karen's words.

"Sure. I'll use last week's *Mountain Times* weekly, we have some leftover copies."

Jemma groaned as she read the article. It implied that Jemma saw someone park at Karen's neighbor's house and walk up. Tucker would see this. His boss would, too. There went the job offer. Tucker's got to be disappointed in her. Karen must have mis-heard her, or did she?

"Something wrong?" Bob asked.

"Huh? Not really. Mind if I take this newspaper?"

Bob's eyes widened. "That's right. You had something to do with that fire up in Hickory Hills yesterday. You were first on the scene, weren't you? Take the paper. We've already read it. We'll save you the *High Country Press* when it comes out tomorrow."

"No thanks. We get copies of the free weeklies at the ranch. Our *Watauga Democrat* comes in the mail a few days late."

"So does ours. One of our customers left this one that he'd picked up in town this morning." Bob carried the box to the cash register. Jemma wrote a ranch check then tucked the newspaper into the box. "Will we see you again before we close?"

"Probably not. Have a warm winter down south."

Jemma loaded the box in the cab of the truck and drove to her workshop at Lottie's.

DETECTIVES TUCKER AND GRAVES spent the first hour of the morning going through the files from the busted locked drawers in the guest-house office while an SBI officer went through the victim's computer files. Some entries dated back to the year she moved to Watauga County, including notes on the former sheriff and a couple of judges. Most of the information was innocuous, not fodder for blackmail. Some involved a tally sheet of favors. The lady played for power but wasn't that good at it. She couldn't even get the state to take over road maintenance in the subdivision.

"Tucker, get in here!"

Tucker sprung to his feet and was in the chief's office in a split second.

"Have you seen this?" She thrust the *Watauga Democrat* in front of his face.

"Not yet."

"Read it now." The chief sat and drilled him with her eyes as he quickly scanned the front page article.

"I didn't talk to the press. They were never at the crime scene."

"Isn't this the Jemma Chase who interviewed in Communications? Aren't you dating her?"

"Yes to both questions, but I didn't tell her anything. I took her statement last night. She's been doing carpentry work for the Karen mentioned in the article. She may have told her some things."

"Doesn't she have sense enough to keep her mouth shut? Find out about this Karen Harmon." The chief leaned back in her chair. "What do you have so far?"

"The victim set the fire. We found a letter she wrote to the property owners in the development citing the fire and earlier break-in as reason for a special assessment to pave the road. The letter is dated for tomorrow. It looks like she went back into the guest house and fell. The autopsy is scheduled for ten this morning so we'll know more after that."

"That's it?"

"All homeowners had a file in the cabinet except one, the Harmons."

"Not much of a lead but follow up. Any conflict of interest because of Jemma Chase?"

"Not as far as I'm concerned. We all have a heavy case load." Most didn't involve bodily injury and could wait. He'd met and talked to Petula and Jemma'd made a heroic effort to save her, bringing the case closer to his own life.

"Do this strictly by procedure. Keep me informed."

Tucker stopped by his desk for a jacket. He told Graves what happened.

"Glad I wasn't there, but why wasn't I included?"

"My guess is because I know Jemma. She may have expected to ream me out for telling her something. But I didn't tell Jemma anything and the chief calmed down."

"Didn't tell her anything? You have more will power than I did when I first met my wife. Women are curious as kinfolk." Graves put on his jacket and winter gloves.

"She's curious as those cats of hers. I don't raise to the bait."

The computer specialist was still working on the Windsor computer when Tucker and Graves left for the morgue in the hospital basement. They waited for the medical examiner to finish and give them a verbal report. The written report would follow a few months after the Chief Medical Examiner's office in Chapel Hill reviewed them.

"Mrs. Windsor did not die from smoke inhalation. It was a blow to the back of the head with a blunt object." The doctor stripped off his gloves. "That changes things, I understand. No way it was an accident."

"She was face up when found. Thanks, doctor." Tucker watched the doctor leave before saying anything to Graves. "Clues go cold so fast. We're running out of time. Let's have a chat with Karen Harmon."

"I want to talk to the brother this afternoon," Graves said.

"We'll make up a list of suspects, including the husband," Tucker said. All the other cases went on hold the minute this one became a homicide. Mentally, Tucker shifted away from nagging thoughts, loose ends and puzzles concerning those cases to a focus on one project – the who and why of the Windsor case.

Graves hesitated then asked, "Including Jemma?"

Tucker nodded. "Normal procedure." He turned on the engine and faced Graves. "Should I pull myself off this case?"

"I don't think so but we'll leave it up to the chief."

Traffic was light so the trip to Hickory Hills didn't take long.

"Excuse the mess, detectives. I'm having part of my kitchen remodeled. I have a wonderful cabinet maker. Maybe you've heard of her, Jemma Chase." Mrs. Karen Harmon snapped her gum. "Sit, sit. We can be comfortable over by the fireplace." She punched a remote control with a bright red fingernail and the gas fire sprang into being. "I do love a fire, don't you?"

"Mrs. Harmon –" Tucker began. The woman was a hummingbird, non-stop motion. She hadn't changed since high school.

"Gosh, Tucker, please call me Karen."

Tucker nodded, then continued, "We're here about Petula Windsor."

"Oh." She almost swallowed her gum. "I didn't mean it like that. Terrible shame what happened to her. I was just chattering, like my husband claims I do."

"What did you think of her?"

"Bless her heart, she meant well. I couldn't go along with her POA philosophy, though."

"What do you mean?"

"I didn't hate her, mind you, I just wanted her to quit picking on us neighbors. I'm for standards in the development, but not ones changed to fit her personal desires." Her fingers tapped her collar bone. "How I do go on."

"Could you give us an example?"

"She argued against cutting down a tree that was struck by lightening and strips of bark had blown off. The POA regulations say that all trees over six inches cannot be cut without approval, you see. Another time, she wanted to fine someone for selling off a collection of Star Trek memorabilia on eBay, calling that a commercial enterprise. He wasn't setting up an office or anything."

"Do you know why she acted that way?"

Karen nodded. "She loved power. She admired those that had it. The best she could do was POA president. You see, most people won't volunteer to do the work. Some are too busy; some don't care. You know people like that, right?"

"Yes. Anything else?"

"She snatched her place at the top of the mountain at an auction for a tenth of what it was worth and inflated her vision for this area. Honey, she bought a large house, then added on two wings a couple of years later."

"What were you planning to do about her?" Tucker asked while Graves continued taking notes.

"Vote her out at the upcoming meeting. See, I've contacted all the land owners who don't live here year-round and never come to meetings. Many of them sent me their proxy votes. I'll be president. I don't trust the vice president. He went along with whatever Petula wanted. She had that effect on men," she said with mischief in her eyes.

"Will that give you enough votes?"

"Add those to the women who have influence on their husbands. We were tired of her ways. Don't get me wrong, I like a little flirting as well as the next woman, but she took it too far."

"What will happen at the meeting now?"

"I don't know. I'm not on the current board. I was the sole person willing to go against her. Only now, all the fun's gone out of it. I'll still do a good job, if it comes to that, but the challenge is gone."

"Did you see any strange cars driving up the road?"

"No, but I only look out the window occasionally. I haven't seen anyone park at the neighbors, either." She pointed up the road.

"What made you say that?"

"I thought you were going to ask me that question. Jemma did."

You then told the reporters, Tucker thought before standing. He held off asking about the missing file until the computer files had been examined. "If you think of anything else, give me a call at this number." He handed her a card and they left.

"Jemma strikes again," Graves said as Tucker parallel parked the car a block from Perfect for Framing. Odds were against a closer parking space on the busy street. They found Mrs. Dixon in her office at the back of the shop. Part store room, part supply closet, the office was over-crowded but neat. "Mrs. Dixon, we're Detectives Tucker and Graves," Tucker said as he closed the door behind him. "We'd like to talk to you about Petula Windsor." One more person would not have fit in the space.

"I heard about her death."

"From?"

"A friend who lives in the development." Mrs. Dixon closed the folder she had been working on when they arrived. "Bungled arson, wasn't it?"

Slight mountain accent, basically organized office, smart-casual clothing clicked in Tucker's mind. "We can't say, ma'am. May we call you Ann?" At her nod, Tucker continued. "How did you know her?"

"She was president of the Property Owners Association in the development where I'm building a house."

"How did you get along with her?" Tucker asked the questions while Graves noted down the responses. The area was so tight Tucker stood with hands clasp in front, legs nearly touching the desk and his back against the door.

Ann shifted in her chair. "I didn't know her very well. My contractor had more contact with her than I did."

"Did you attend any POA meetings with her?"

One of her eyebrows twitched. "One when my late husband and I first bought the lot and one many months ago. I wanted to have a chance to meet some of my neighbors before I moved to the development. Most were friendly and I already know one of the people who live there, Karen Harmon."

"What happened at the second meeting?"

Ann blinked a number of times. "Petula's move to have a one-time fee to pave the road failed. An announcement was made for the building committee to meet sometime after that." Her voice constricted.

"Anything else?"

"As you've probably heard, she provoked me and I hit her."

Tucker had a quick visual image of the two women fighting. "What happened?"

Ann gave her account, complete with venom in her voice.

"When was the last time you saw Petula?" Tucker leaned in and put both hands on the desk, locking his eyes with hers.

"Jemma Chase put you up to this, didn't she?" Ann slapped the desk with her palm. "All right, I saw Petula yesterday morning. She was in the guest house and I took another copy of my house plans to her. She'd claimed that she lost the copies even though my real estate agent personally handed them to her. I also gave her one." She took a deep breath before continuing. "She was suing me because my contractor had cleared the house site and put in a well and septic. Her time to decline the plans had run out and she still delayed approval."

"What time was this?"

"A quarter past twelve. I knew she'd be home since that was her habit."

"How did you know her habits?"

"Karen lives there."

"How long did the meeting last?"

"All of five minutes. She threw me out." Ann rose from the chair, keeping eye contact with Tucker.

Tucker felt a growing strength of will from the woman. "Did anyone see the two of you together?"

"No. Wait." Her tough stance softened. "Jemma saw me leave, as she probably told you. Look, I thought this was accidental death. Why are you asking me these questions?"

"We're tracing her last day. Did you have your car serviced recently?"

"Last week. Why?"

"Thank you." Tucker and Graves left as Ann sank back into her chair.

Jemma, intending to stay only a minute, stuck her head in to say hello to Lottie before starting in the workshop. Aunt Alma's lesson in manners had stuck. Truth be told, Jemma liked Lottie and hoped to live to be such an independent old lady.

"Lawd, child, come in here. Tell me the details the paper left out."

"I'm not supposed to talk about it. I slipped up yesterday and now it's all over the county. Did you know I've interviewed for a job at the sheriff's department?" Jemma stepped inside, closed the door but kept her hand on the knob.

"No, I didn't know that. Why would a girl like you want to work there?" Lottie sat by the heater and motioned for Jemma to join her.

Jemma shook her head.

"What do you mean?" If she thinks I can't solve a mystery, she doesn't know me very well, Jemma thought.

"You're your own boss. You work with your hands." Lottie rocked a couple of times. "You take pictures. Then there's the horses, which I know you love. Would you give all that up?" She stopped rocking.

Jemma's defense faded. "It'd be steady money. I want to work up to being an investigator. You know, go around solving crimes."

"If you ask me, it don't fit you."

Jemma felt like a kid whose balloon popped.

"Never mind me, I sometimes talk without thinking. I guess that means you're keeping quiet about what you know."

"I'm sorry, Miz Lottie. I messed up and told one person and it ended up in the papers. I sort of promised the detective." Squirming under Lottie's questions and opinions, Jemma turned the door knob to escape.

"It'll all come out in time. You staying for lunch? It'll be noon shortly."

"Thanks, but not today. I missed yesterday afternoon and I'm facing a deadline."

Jemma went into the workshop, fed the wood stove and felt relieved that she'd only lost a few minutes. She knew Karen needed the corner cabinet as soon as possible. Jemma built the frame but her mind kept returning to yesterday. She measured twice, then cut the side with a table saw. The fit was perfect. Inhaling the smoke was bad enough, but imagine dying from it? Struggling for air, coughing up soot. Why was she face up? If she'd tried to crawl her way out, she would have been on her knees.

Chapter 10

$\mathcal{D}$ETECTIVES TUCKER AND GRAVES drove to Raymond Viccaro's house. Patches of dirt dotted the brown lawn, the siding needed painting, the railing was down on one side of the porch. The doorbell didn't work. He sure lived differently than his sister.

"Sorry to hear about your loss," Graves said once they were inside. "We'd like to ask you a few questions about your sister. You were real close?"

"She's – was – my step-sister. She was older than me and took me under her wing, so to speak, early on. We had a unique relationship." Ray motioned them to sit. "After my second divorce a few years ago, I moved into this rental house with another guy. She found it for me. Pet helped me through a difficult period and I would have done anything for her. She even set me up with a couple of dates. Okay if I smoke?" He held up a pack of cigarettes and Tucker nodded.

Ray took a deep drag and leaned back in the chair. "She found me this job. Never been one like her before, never will be again."

"Where were you yesterday morning between nine and one in the afternoon?"

"I know where I wish I'd been. With my sister. Maybe I could have saved her." He blinked red-rimmed eyes several times.

"Where were you?"

Ray sat up. "Why? What has this got to do with her accident?"

"We're calling it a homicide."

He took another puff then stubbed out the butt in an over-filled ash tray. "Maybe I should get a lawyer."

"That's your choice."

"I was here, then went to lunch at Wendy's around noon. You should talk to Travis Miller, a mechanic where I work." He stood. "He's had a grudge against my sister for ten years. He likes fire." His lower jaw jutted out.

"That'll be all for now." Graves led the way out to the car and frowned when Ray slammed the door behind them. "He acted genuine enough about missing his sister. Do we have anything on Travis Miller?"

"Not yet." Tucker, an only child, tried to imagine losing a sibling. He shuddered at the thought of even losing a cousin.

"What say we grab a bite at Wendy's, then head back to the office. Something may have turned up on the computer files."

Jemma was absorbed in fitting the upper doors for the glass panes when she had a visitor.

"I hear you had a close call yesterday."

Jemma squealed and jumped. "You scared me, sneaking up like that." She'd been so focused on her work that she hadn't heard him come into the workshop.

Travis grinned, then squatted down to stabilize the base of the cabinet while she drilled a starter hole.

"It happened so fast I didn't have time to worry about it." Jemma screwed in a screw. "Thanks." A second pair of hands was appreciated on occasion.

"Good thing you was there. Fire could have spread to this side of the mountain. Mamaw could have lost all those trees, even this house. We'd a been living in my car if it hadn't been for you."

"I'm sure Ward would have found the fire soon enough." She moved to another corner of the cabinet and drilled a hole.

"Not if he set the whole thing up."

"What do you mean?" She screwed in another piece of wood.

"It was murder. The sheriff's men talked with Mrs. Windsor's brother at the shop this morning. He told the cashier who told the parts department lady whose cousin is the head mechanic. It's got to be true."

Jemma laid down the screw driver and stood. "That so?" Murder. Ward was at the house and could have easily started the fire providing the means. Why? The simple answer was jealousy. This morning she'd seen her male kitty attack the female because Jemma petted her a long time, only she was strong enough to hiss and fight back.

"Yes, ma'am. If there's ever anything I can do for you, just holler." Travis stood, patted her shoulder and went to the door. "I mean that. You have trouble with your truck, I'm your man. You need help loading these cabinets, let me know. You wanna go to a movie, say when."

"Thanks, Travis." Was that a come on? Cute kid but he was too late in the romance department.

Jemma spent the afternoon working on the cabinets. Tucker asked her to stay out of the investigation and she would. She'd prove that she could leave the detecting to the investigators. Her job, if she got it, would be communications, not playing CSI. She was fully capable of keeping out of other people's business. The interview went fine and now was not the time to screw things up.

After she reached a good stopping point and picked up the scrap lumber, she selected a few pieces to see if they would go together for a small bird house. She hummed as she measured, sawed, screwed and glued. Once she screwed in an "o" hook in the top, she examined her work. Before applying a coat of polyurethane, she drew the Blue Falls Ranch brand on the back, then signed and dated the piece. This first one took longer than she liked but she'd get faster at the bird houses. Hers was very different from the ones she'd seen at Todd General Store that morning. She hadn't copied someone else's creation but had been inspired by it. She finished cleaning up, satisfied with a productive day.

BACK AT THE SHERIFF's complex, Tucker poured himself a cup of coffee. Just one, he told himself. Jemma claimed caffeine contributed to his sleep problems. "Your Petula collected gossip. Check this out. She had computer files on each family in the POA, other real estate offices, bank employees who work with her husband, people she ran into at the doctor's office. If she heard it, she keyed it in. She kept a separate log sheet of events." The computer expert stood and motioned Tucker to take over his chair. "Where do you want to start?"

"POA." It took Tucker only a few moments to see how to navigate Petula's files. Graves pulled up a chair next to him to take notes. They'd print hard copies to reference later.

Tucker chuckled. "I guess she had something against dogs. She tried to make the owners clean up the urine as well as the poop."

"At least we know who in the development has pets. In case there is ever a cat attack." Graves pointed to a note next to one of the original home owners.

"You have to give it to her, she was thorough. Everything is dated and set in an exact location." Get to know the victim, get to catch the killer; cause and effect; action and reaction.

"She was a bit too compulsive to suit me."

Tucker looked over at Graves' messy desk and at the spot on his shirt. The contrast made him smile briefly. "This could take all day. We'll concentrate on Karen." Following the house purchasing information, Petula had labeled Karen Harmon as someone to keep watch on. Opposed the road paving, anything to do with controlling animals even though she didn't have any, and had a clear view of the road from her kitchen window. Happily married, two grown children, financial problems due to the children's college expenses. Three overdrawn checks in the past two years. "Ward" was in parentheses. Ally of Ann Dixon. Maneuvering to become the POA president.

Tucker highlighted and printed the Karen Harmon information then went on to Ann Dixon's file. It was easier to pick out the folder and print than take notes. Petula had files on her brother and her husband. Travis and Lottie Miller. Her boss and his wife. "'Darryl Johnson's shady practices' is the title of this file. Let me read some of it to you. 'Failure to disclose right of way on land' and 'Failure to disclose fire damage.' She has dates and names. Let's print this."

"Was she blackmailing him?" Graves wrote "blackmail" in bold letters.

"Why, partner, whatever gave you that idea?" Tucker paused. "Could be why there was a break-in. He could have been worried about what was in the PI report. Let's go back to the original break-in. What if the PI report wasn't the real target? Or the only target?"

"The person went back for more."

"Take Darryl. Suppose he'd spotted someone outside at the guest house and figured it was a PI hired by the husband. He gets the report. Say Petula started blackmailing him after he splits with her. He needs to find what else she has on him."

"Embezzlement maybe."

"From his own company." Tucker shook his head. "Lying to the IRS would be more like it."

"But the Johnson file was still in the cabinet."

"Maybe he took out the incriminating evidence and left the rest."

"Maybe he was caught in the act, ran after Petula, knocked her over the head and started the fire as a cover-up."

"Possibly. But why is Karen Harmon's file missing?"

"A ruse to throw us off. Mis-direction."

"Or to protect her. There wasn't much in her computer file.

The other folders had more in them than had been keyed in the computer."

Graves groaned. "Let's go back to Petula."

Tucker flipped to another screen. "Looks like Petula was planning to frame Ann Dixon for threatening her. She cut out the anonymous note from art magazines, hoping we'd trace them back to the store. She kept meticulous details, almost as if she had some compulsive disorder."

"We hadn't made it that far," Graves admitted.

"She also knew about the proxy votes and Karen's plans to take over the POA. She'd underlined certain phrases like 'over drawn checks' and 'college expenses.' Do you think she was gathering ammunition?"

"I wouldn't put it past her."

"She's even started one on Jemma," Tucker said. It didn't have much, just jobs she done recently and comments.

"What next?" Graves asked.

"Let's see what her boss thinks of her." Tucker called Star Lite Properties and told Darryl to come to the sheriff's complex and then alerted the chief and Graves about the upcoming interrogation. The chief decided to watch the proceeding through the mirror even though the session would be video taped. Tucker walked the hall to the interview room and tried to see the complex through the eyes of a suspect. The two interrogation rooms were side by side, eight by ten feet with mottled gray carpet and off white walls. Each had a two by three foot mirror which allowed the chief to watch from her office. A square gray table had a black chair with its back against the mirrored wall. A metal bench with two welded loops for handcuffing prisoners sat against a perpendicular wall, allowing an upper corner camera a clear view of the interview.

Tucker met Darryl in reception. A locked sliding glass window separated the clerk from the waiting room. Guests spoke into a microphone; the clerk alerted the detective by phone.

"This is my wife, Flora. We only had one car at the office."

Tucker nodded at her. "Ma'am." Petula had described her as an overweight frumpy mother of four grown kids. She looked neglected and sad to Tucker. He led them along a bank of framed photographs of past sheriffs, many wearing cowboy hats. "I'd like to ask you a few questions about Petula Windsor."

"I'll wait outside," Flora said in a brassy voice.

Old Florida accent. Probably says "Miam*a*." "Detective Graves would like to speak with you, Flora. If you will accompany him to this room," Tucker said as they came to the first room, "Darryl and I can talk next door." Tucker had Darryl sit on the bench and Tucker rounded the table to sit against the back wall. "Where were you yesterday from ten to one?"

"I was with my wife."

"Petula's death has been declared a homicide. Would you mind telling me where you were?"

"We met in the Boone Mall Parking lot, around back." Darryl frowned.

"And then what?"

"We sat in the car and talked."

"Did anyone see you?"

"How should I know? We parked out of the way and were, um, involved so I didn't notice anyone. No one approached the car, if that's what you mean." Darryl glared at Tucker. "Now see here. You don't suspect either one of us, do you?" Darryl rose from the bench.

"We're following up on leads. Considering the Windsor's break-in earlier, we need to rule you out. We understand that Petula was blackmailing you." Tucker decided to be direct and blunt with this suspect.

"Why would you say that? I told you about the bracelet. I didn't want my wife to know about the affair." Darryl leaned against the wall but didn't look at Tucker.

"What about other women?" Tucker watched for a flinch, a twitch or a nervous outburst.

"There weren't any other women. She was the first and only."

"Did you know that Petula had a diary of sorts where she listed tidbits of information in tidy files?"

Darryl licked his lips. "What kind of information?"

"Details about real estate transactions that are shady, to say the least. A series of phone calls to and from a couple of different women, times you were unaccounted for during office hours."

"Look. Don't tell my wife. She's starting to forgive me. What she doesn't know won't hurt."

His concern was about his wife rather than the business. "Was Petula blackmailing you?"

Darryl nodded.

Tucker was about to press for more details when Graves knocked and motioned from the doorway. They compared statements and let Flora join her husband on the bench.

"My wife knows all about the contents of that report." Darryl took his wife's hand. "We're coming to terms with my … indiscretion."

"We need some clarification," Tucker said. "The report says you were at the guest house for only fifteen minutes. That's not much warm up time."

Flora frowned, let go of her husband's hand, stood and stepped to the side of the table.

"I was nervous. I planned to end it after," her husband said.

"End it? You couldn't do it then so you went back and took care of her on Tuesday." Tucker leaned into the table.

"No. That's not what happened." Sweat glistened on Darryl's upper lip.

"Exactly what did happen after the cork was popped on the bottle of champagne?" Flora in the room could be a bonus.

Gasp. Flora's wide-eyed implied question sent her back a couple of steps.

"Sweetheart, she brought the champagne. Not me."

Darryl reached out a hand to his wife but she ignored it. Detective Graves brought her a chair from the other interrogation room, then pointed to Tucker, indicating this was his show.

Darryl rapped the desk with his knuckles. "You saw the pictures. You tell me."

"You had sex for two minutes, got dressed, and gave her a gift. Then what?"

"Gift?" Flora's brassy voice turned tinny.

"I told her it was over and left."

Flora didn't react to the sex but to the gift. Interesting. "Didn't she slap you?"

"She may have. I don't remember."

"Your story was different last time. How do you explain that?"

"It happened so fast. I was glad it was over."

"Why don't we add blackmail to Petula's credentials? We can skip over the shady practices of only showing your own listings or claiming someone else's property is under contract when it wasn't."

"You can't be talking about me." Darryl's neck turned red. He turned to his wife but she wasn't interested. She stared at the mirror and sat up straight.

"She struck it big when she discovered that you used deposit money supposedly held in trust to pay for landscaping and an elaborate entrance gate to your new subdivision."

"That's slander. Flora, he's making this up." His puppy dog demeanor pleaded with his wife.

Now for his shot in the dark. "The gift to Petula was a payoff that you could charge and not pay for until after you found a different bank to finance your project."

"You can't prove any of this."

Bingo. "A search warrant to investigate your financial records shouldn't be hard to get."

"You're bluffing." Darryl's face turned a deeper shade of red.

"My version is this. You found out about the report. You broke into Ward's study and stole it. You went to Petula and had another fight. You set fire to the guest house to cover it up."

"No, that's not true. I never saw her alone again."

"How do we know this version of your actions on Tuesday morning is accurate?"

Flora looked down at the floor.

"We were together." Darryl looked at his wife.

"Flora, do you have anything to add?"

She shook her head but didn't look at them.

"We were together. That's all you need to know," Darryl repeated.

"For now," Tucker said as they left. "You could have asked a few questions back there."

Graves walked beside Tucker. "And broken your rhythm? You scored a direct hit with the subdivision financing."

"Thanks. I want to take another look at the crime scene."

"Me, too. A light snow's in this evening's forecast," Graves said while driving through Boone, past New Market Center, along Hwy 194 and turning into Hickory Hills.

Once there, Tucker remarked, "This is the only road up here. The nearest house is five hundred feet down the mountain."

"The gravel and steepness rule out a bicycle. Someone could have parked at the house below and walked up. We know the private investigator walked further than that."

"Do you want to check with the neighbor while I keep looking up here?"

Graves left and Tucker walked all the way around the guest house. He looked in the garage window. Petula's car was in the garage but Ward's wasn't. He slowed when he approached the back porch. The temperature was dropping and some of the standing water from the fire hose had frozen. He looked through the trees to the long-range view, then walked on over the ridge and into the woods. Following a deer trail, he came to a triangular feeder attached to a tree. Scouting around, he spotted a deer stand, fully camouflaged, fifteen feet off the ground. Not far in front of it was an old logging trail. A few snowflakes fell and he returned to the car.

"The neighbors weren't home. I didn't see anything in their driveway. What about you?"

Tucker told Graves about the hunting setup.

Chapter 11

*J*EMMA LEFT THE workshop with light snow falling. It didn't take but ten minutes to drive down, around and then up the mountain to the Windsor house. Ward greeted her at the door and led her to his study. Finally, she'd see the scene of the break-in. Books, books and more books caught her attention but nothing seemed out of place. It had been over a week. What did she expect?

"Have a seat. This won't take long if I can find my check book. The sheriff's people were all over my desk this morning."

His face was wan. Jemma thought about what it would feel like to lose Tucker, and they'd only been together for a few months. Ward would have to rebuild his whole life outside work. He'd have to learn to cook and learn to eat in a restaurant alone. How would he spend his evenings? Eventually, he'd have to date, unless he already had a woman in mind. "I'm sorry about this. I feel so dumb for washing the check."

"It's the least of my concerns right now."

"I didn't have a chance to offer my condolences."

He looked at her, almost said something, then shook his

head. "Here it is." He pulled out a big notebook, the kind used by businesses, with four checks on a page. The phone rang while he wrote the check. "Hello."

A number of photos of Petula lay on the corner of his desk. When he saw Jemma look at them, he put a notepad on top. She read "POA members" on the pad with check marks beside the first few names. "Can we discuss this another time?" he said to the caller. "You have all the money you're going to get. You bungled the job." He hung up and looked at Jemma. "Landscape company." He finished writing the check and handed it to her. "Would you be interested in rebuilding the porch on the guest house? I have a clean up-crew lined up for the smoke damage inside."

"It would be a couple of weeks before I could get to it."

"I consider that a yes. I'd like it done as soon as possible."

The weather and Christmas might push it into the new year but she'd think about that when the time came. "Don't get up. I can see myself out," Jemma said. Partway down the hall, she heard a strange noise. She walked back to the study and was about to say something, then stopped and stared at Ward shredding his wife's photos.

Petula thought she had Ward trained, over-trained, Jemma imagined. Petula acted as though she possessed him. How could a person ever really know another person? Possession and jealousy, twin emotions that hurt everyone involved. Jemma wouldn't let her interest in Tucker go to that extreme, not after this.

That evening on the phone as Tucker leaned back in his easy chair, letting Jemma's voice flow through him, she began with something Tucker wanted to hear.

"I know I promised to keep out of this so I'm going to unload all my ideas and let you deal with them."

"That's a wise decision. Let me have it." Tucker glanced out the window, hoping the snow fall would be light.

"I think Ward Windsor killed his own wife."

"Based on what evidence?" He'd already dismissed him as a suspect. Call it gut feeling but the man had put up with her for many years.

"Jealousy was the motive. She may have thought she had him well trained but he surprised her. He also wanted to take over the POA but didn't dare confront her. He had a list of the members he was working on in his office when I saw him today."

Tucker's stomach tightened. "Why did you see him?"

Jemma explained about the check. "When I left, I glanced back and he was shredding all his wife's photos." She told him about the phone call. "Landscape company, my eye. You should have heard his tone of voice."

Tucker again relaxed. "He did write a check to the landscape company, according to his records. He was probably contacting the property owners to let them know about the funeral arrangements. You don't have much of a case."

"Oh, well ..."

"C-Girl, let it go. Tell you what, I'll visit him again day after tomorrow. The funeral's tomorrow and he has enough to do without me coming around. Will that satisfy you?"

"I guess it'll have to. He's hired me to rebuild his porch. Do you want me to cancel on that?"

"No. But keep your paws on the porch and leave the investigation to this Gator."

"Did anything exciting happen today?"

"Did you hear about the lockdown on ASU campus tonight? It's not my case but a student entered his house just off campus and interrupted a robbery. The six foot tall man in a ski mask and Pink Floyd T-shirt was stealing his television. The man had a gun so the student slammed the door, ran and called the police. The armed robber ran through the woods to campus and is still at large."

"Pink Floyd T-shirt. The comedians will love the image, especially since no one was hurt. That reminds me, did you hear anything about my interview? It's been over a week."

113

"The chief's still interviewing. Like she told you, it isn't a quick process. Patience. This job takes patience." Tucker cleared his throat. "Want to tell me exactly what you told Karen Harmon?"

"Oh, Tucker, I'm so sorry. I was rattled from the fire and she flagged me down on my way home. I told her about the fire and asked if she'd seen someone parked next door. I did not say that I'd seen someone."

"They could pull me from the case because of this." Tucker winked at Jemma's photo, knowing the case belonged to him and Graves and grabbed the chance to caution Jemma yet again.

"I promise not to say anything to anyone, except you. Give me another chance."

"We'll see. How are DT and JK?"

"Showing signs of jealousy. When I pet one, the other one wants attention. Sometimes they do these little mock fights, like power plays. They follow me around like dogs. I'm part of their territory now. Holding onto possessions, alive or inert, must be innate in all animals."

Chapter 12
THURSDAY

*J*EMMA DROVE UP the mountain, through a cloud of fog and into a light mist. The day was gray when she passed the Welcome to Boone sign. She looked for Tucker at the burial site on Thursday morning. It was spitting snow at the higher elevation and the temperature hovered around freezing. She'd read in the *High Country Press* that the service started at eleven. A large canopy kept the site, pastor and some visitors dry. Standing in the back of the small crowd, she listened to the pastor speak briefly about Petula Windsor and how much she would be missed. It lasted all of three minutes. As people left the service, many of them said a few words to Ward. Ann and Karen were in the informal line in front of Jemma but she didn't call attention to herself.

Jemma heard Ward say to Ann, "I've stayed out of Petula's POA business, but I plan to go over her notes this week and give a recommendation to the group. I'll be at the meeting."

"I'm sorry about your loss. I would appreciate your help with approving the plans to get my house built," Ann said before moving on.

"Thank you for coming, Karen. I know you fought with

Petula over the POA, but she was a good woman in a way."

Jemma had a clear view above Karen's head of Ward's tired eyes. Had he been worried about getting caught? Did his conscience bother him? Did he regret killing his wife?

"I'm sorry for your loss," Karen said.

Jemma mumbled her condolences and stepped aside before spotting Detective Tucker in a dark suit a couple of yards away from the canopy. "Short service, don't you think?" Jemma asked him in a whisper. She dusted the snow off his shoulder.

Tucker nodded but kept still, watching each person who approached Ward.

"Who's that on the other side of the casket?" Jemma kept her voice low, noticing some people greeting Ward.

"The deceased's stepbrother."

"Who's that talking with him?"

"Her boss and his wife, Darryl and Flora Johnson."

Jemma thought she recognized the woman from the Perfect for Framing shop. The broker and wife came around the grave site and spoke to Ward. Darryl said, "I'm sorry about your loss. She was a good office manager."

Ward's face turned red but he kept his voice low. "How dare you show up here? After what you did to her."

Darryl stalked away with his wife striding to catch up with him.

Jemma looked at Tucker. He shook his head. The stepbrother didn't approach Ward and they never said a word to each other. Jemma followed Tucker after the service was over and all the guests were gone.

"What was that all about?" Jemma asked. Had she been wrong? Did Darryl and or his wife strike Petula?

"You don't need to know." Tucker kept walking.

"Gator?" She grabbed his hand and stopped him.

"You can't tell anyone – not Alma, not Lottie, not Karen, not even Brandy. You understand?" He looked her straight in the eyes, his face grim.

Jemma nodded and didn't smile. A snowflake hit her eyelashes so she blinked.

Tucker walked to Jemma's truck. "Petula had an affair with her boss."

"That's terrible." Jemma wiped her hands on her pants as if she were dirtied by the knowledge. "What —"

"No more details. I'm the investigator and you're not. Remember?"

Jemma stifled a grumble. Back to Ward as her main suspect. "How about lunch? We both have to eat." Jemma looked around. "Where's Graves?"

"He's going over files. Dos Amigos?"

Jemma climbed into her truck. "I can change into my work clothes in their bathroom."

Over chicken fajitas cooked and served by authentic Mexicans Jemma told Tucker all she knew about the people on her list of suspects, hoping for reciprocation. "The husband is always the first suspect. The lover is second. Don't forget Flora, the vengeful wife of Darryl. Then there is Ann, wronged property owner who is determined to build her dead husband's dream house."

"What about Travis? Remember what Alma said about mountain wrongs aren't forgotten."

"I'd hate for it to be Travis. It would be the end of Lottie. Maybe it's someone in the POA who was tired of her petty power plays." Jemma spooned the chicken, pepper and onion concoction onto a flour tortilla, folded it and bit into it. Half the contents fell back onto her plate.

"Petty Petula? What about sharp-eyed Karen?"

"Treacherous Travis or Dangerous Darryl." Jemma couldn't think of one for Flora. "Raging Ray." She resorted to eating the spicy mixture with her fork and tearing off bits of the tortilla and eating them separately.

"Enough already." Tucker emptied his glass of sweet tea and put it at the back of the table, indicating that he didn't need a refill.

"I vote for the husband. Jealousy is a strong motive." When

117

he didn't offer any details about the case, Jemma went to change clothes in the restaurant bathroom. They walked out together, promising each other a phone call that evening.

Tucker met Detective Graves at the Sheriff's complex, waiting for Travis to arrive from the Ford dealership. Snow had dusted trees and bushes but didn't stick to the roads. "When are you going to get a new suit?"

Tucker undid the two buttons on his jacket. "When this one wears out."

When Travis arrived, Tucker led him to one of the interrogation rooms. "Have a seat. We have a few more questions." Tucker sat in the black chair. Graves leaned against the door.

Travis pulled a shop towel from his back pocket and wiped his hands then sat on the metal bench. "I don't know but what I read in the paper."

"Is that your hunting stand at the top of the ridge?"

Travis re-wiped his hands. "Yeah. I pay for a license every year. I only shoot my limit."

"Do you sit in the stand off season?"

"You have to watch their habits. Deer and turkey are not that easy to get." Travis rested his hands on the table.

"You like to study on them. What about people? Do you like to study on them?" Tucker kept his voice even.

"What are you gettin' at?" Travis glanced at the mirror.

"Petula's guest house is a two-minute walk from your stand." Tucker let the insinuation hang in the air.

"What? You think I spied on her?" Travis shook his head. "I kept as far away from her as I could."

"From what I hear, you had an old grudge against her. Didn't she practically steal that land from your family?"

"Not much I can do about that," Travis grumbled.

"So you play little tricks on her brother." Graves sneered down at him, almost jeering at the young man.

"What do you mean?" Travis glanced at Graves then at the camera in the upper corner of the room. He sat up straight and put his hands under the table.

"Cartoons, putting inappropriate magazines on his desk. Need I go on?"

"I was just funning him. It didn't do no harm."

"I understand you have a history with fire."

Red crept up Travis' neck. "That was a frame-up. I didn't know anything about that until the sheriff came to the house. She set me up."

"Claiming not to know isn't a defense. Then you were a kid, but now, you're fair game."

"I was out doing errands that day. Boss had me pick up some washer fluid on sale. I went to the drug store for Mamaw, bought socks at Wal-Mart, batteries too. Grabbed a sandwich at Subway."

"Do you have any receipts?" Graves interjected.

"Boss has his. Maybe Mamaw has hers from the drug store."

"Still, you'd have time to do that and get to Hickory Hills and back." Tucker doubted he'd get more out of this subject today. "Don't leave town, you hear?" Tucker let Graves escort Travis out. People tended to fall back on old habits. If fire had worked once, it could work again.

Detectives Tucker and Graves next visited Karen Harmon in Hickory Hills.

"Excuse the mess. I'm having part of my kitchen redone. I do have coffee." Karen led them to the living room.

Tucker looked toward the kitchen. "No thanks on the coffee. Do you have any gum? I had onions at lunch."

"Here you are," she said, opening her purse. "Take two. I always add a second after a few minutes. Would you like to see the cabinets?" She took them to the breakfast bar. "Jemma Chase does fine work, don't you think?"

Tucker popped one piece of gum in his mouth and pocketed the wrapper and second piece then ran his hands over the inlaid wood counter top. "Yes, ma'am. We stopped by to find out what you thought about Petula Windsor."

Karen's gum chewing slowed down. "She was not one of my favorites. Most of us property owners want to have a POA with minimum fuss. We need one to pay for plowing the road in winter, for getting gravel put down. We want a certain standard for house construction but she wanted way too much."

"What do you mean?"

"People build in here to retire or to have second homes. She wanted to change the standards so that only the wealthy could build. I don't agree with that." Karen tilted her head. "With the men, Petula could use her body as a tool. Flirting, making a guy feel young again." She winked for emphasis. "That wouldn't work with us women."

"Did she flirt with your husband?"

"She did. I told her to lay off, in no uncertain terms. I told her she'd regret it if she didn't leave all the men in this development alone. I'd fight her with all I could."

"How?" Tucker caught himself gliding his fingers over the smooth curved edge of the breakfast bar and picturing Jemma sanding every inch.

"Not by killing her, if that's what you're thinking." Karen snapped her gum. "I've talked with the other wives and we've banded together and planned to block everything she wanted at the meeting this Saturday. I plan to be the next president. Only now, I doubt anyone will bring up the changes."

"Are you still having the meeting?" Tucker asked, still admiring the craftmanship of the breakfast bar.

"We have to. Some owners drive up here from Florida, Myrtle Beach. One from Ohio."

Tucker kept it casual. "Will you get your wish and become president?"

"I expect so."

"Did you know that Petula kept files on everyone in the development?"

Karen snapped her gum a couple of times. "I'm not surprised.

She would bring up things that happened long ago at the meetings. I can imagine what was in my file, especially since I planned to take over as president." Karen hesitated, then asked, "What was in my file?"

"We don't know. It's missing." Tucker interjected wonder in his voice.

"I didn't take it if that's what you're thinking."

"How well do you know Darryl Johnson?"

"He's a friend of Ann's so I see him and Flora on occasion. Why?"

Neither detective said anything.

"Did you hear there was something between us? It's not true. I'd never even think of doing that to my husband."

"What do you know about Ann Dixon?"

"She's a great woman and has been through a lot this past year, with her husband's death. She's determined to build the house he designed."

"How did he die?"

"Heart attack. He was only fifty, a decade older than me. It makes you realize how quickly life can be ended."

JEMMA WAS ABOUT TO turn off the workshop lights when Travis met her at the door. He backed her inside and closed the door. "I got to tell somebody."

Case solved? A confession of murder? Jemma walked to the other side of the work bench to put some distance between them. No telling what he'd do with her after he confessed. "Why me?"

"Mamaw says you're seeing Detective Tucker. He asked me some questions today. He thinks I killed Mrs. Windsor." Travis leaned over the bench. "I didn't, but I know more than I told him. I was hoping that I could tell you and you could tell him. But you'd have to promise not to tell that I'm the one who told you. Promise?"

"Okay." He wouldn't hurt her, would he? She'd already put

all the tools away. Not even a screw driver was at hand.

"You got to swear. If he finds out I know, I'd get real mad."

"I swear." If she yelled, surely Lottie would hear.

Travis paced and talked. "The detective was right about one thing, I did spy on them a few times. I have this deer stand up at the top of the mountain. Sometimes I'd follow the deer trail to where I could use my binoculars to see in the bedroom of the guest house."

"And?"

"Her and her brother were close."

Siblings lend money or loan a car. "How close?"

"Close as dogs in heat."

"Yuck. Wait a minute, he was her step-brother which deserves only a half-yuck," Jemma said to lighten the atmosphere.

"It didn't bother me when she was with her boss, but her own step-kin? That's sick. It keeps playing in my head, like a head worm. It's like a bad tattoo, I can't get rid of the sound or picture."

"Sound?"

"I had to make sure my eyes weren't deceiving me. It drew me in the second time. I watched from the porch." He stopped pacing. "You promised to pass this on without mentioning my name, remember?"

"You can be sure of that."

"I'm gonna trust you. I feel better now. You're not engaged to him or anything, are you?" Travis shook his shoulders and stretched his neck, like a horse moments after the saddle was taken off.

"No."

"Thanks. Maybe we can go out sometime. I best get in to supper."

Jemma left wondering if he was trying to frame the brother. It had stopped snowing and Jemma had a thoughtful drive home.

PERFECT FOR FRAMING was still open by the time Tucker and Graves opened the door. The light snow had continued most of the day but the ground was too warm for it to stick. They went straight back to the office and found Ann Dixon preparing to leave for the evening. She looked up, then continued filling her briefcase with a bank bag, a Saslow jewelers case, papers, and a hairbrush. "What can I do for you?" she asked, then shut the briefcase. She put on her coat and draped a wool scarf over her head.

"We have a few more questions. This won't take long."

"I need to get to the bank." Ann walked through the office door, held it for the detectives, then closed it.

"Did you see anyone besides Petula the day of the fire?"

"No. I did see Ward's car but didn't actually see him." She led them to the front of the store. "On the drive down, I saw Jemma Chase. We've been over this."

"What was your relationship with Petula?"

"Adversarial. She wouldn't approve the house plans my husband drew up." She looked around the store then called out, "We're closing."

"Couldn't you change them to meet her specifications?" Two stubborn people with heels dug in on principle could lead to either a standoff or a fight with a big loser. Ann may have thought she had too much to lose.

"I don't want to. My husband and I spent months designing that house. It's perfect. I didn't want to change a thing. I considered counter-suing the little bully but it was too expensive. I did mail some eight by eleven inch copies of my plans to everyone in the development."

"Why's that?"

"To put pressure on her. I did send a letter to the editor about the abuse of power some of these POAs have. I understand someone mailed her a copy."

No customers came forward so Ann used her key to run a cash register tape and lock up for the night.

"What happened to your husband?"

Her head jerked up from watching the tape. "He died." Ann's voice was flat. She put the tape in her briefcase and commented, "I counted the cash and checks earlier so we can leave now."

"How did he die?"

Her eyebrow twitched. "They said it was a heart attack. By the time I saw him at the hospital, he was dead. He collapsed while drinking coffee at a POA meeting."

They followed Ann out the front door and she locked it. "What has this to do with anything?" She put on her gloves. "Am I a suspect?"

"Thank you for your time, ma'am."

Jemma rushed into the ranch kitchen. "Am I too late to help?"

"Everything's ready. Wash up and join us." Alma backed out the swinging door, hands loaded with two pumpkin pies.

The phone rang and Jemma answered it. After the preliminaries, Jemma's mouth went dry. "You're offering me the job?"

"That's right. We need an answer soon. I understand if you want to think about it. Would you call me on Monday?"

"Yes. I'll know by then." Jemma hung up the phone and drifted into the dining room.

She sat between Bo and Alma, nodded to Randy, Alma's steady, passed bowls of food, and loaded her plate, all without saying a word. The sheriff's department wanted her. The first step toward a life in crime – from the good guys side – was offered and available. Eventually she could carry a badge and a gun. She'd be included in case detail discussions and could put together the puzzle pieces to solve crimes.

Pearle and Lyle Bishop strolled in the door. "Neither of us felt like cooking tonight." Clinton Triplett followed.

"We have room." Bo scooted over his chair. Miguel did the same and three places were added to the round table.

"What's the joke?" Lyle asked after settling in.

The diners looked at each other, puzzled.

"Jemma's got a funny smile on her face."

Jemma blinked and looked around the table. Guests from the other tables stared at her. "I've been offered a job in communications at the sheriff's office."

Half-hearted congratulations greeted her.

"We were expecting news about the murder," Clinton said.

"Sí," Miguel said, then ducked his head.

"Behave yourselves. Are you going to accept?" Alma glared at Clinton before returning her attention to Jemma.

"I don't know. There are lots of things to consider."

"A steady paycheck. Pass the cornbread, please. And the pickled okra." Pearle smiled at Jemma.

As the pickled okra, cornbread and butter traveled around the table, Jemma heard advice, both pro and con, from people at all the tables, from "go for it" to "you'd die being inside all day" to "aren't you afraid of being shot?"

Conversation lulled as people ate. Alma and Jemma cleared away the plates while everyone helped themselves to coffee and pie from the sideboard.

"I heard the POA board got together and decided she had to go." Randy added a dollop of homemade whipped cream to his slice of pie.

"Permanently?"

Clinton frowned, whether about the conversation or which piece of pie, Jemma didn't know.

"I doubt they voted on it or meant for her to be killed. Bet they are happy, though." Randy brought Alma a piece and was rewarded with a wide-eyed smile.

Bo said, "According to TV, the husband's always top suspect. I bet he did it."

"It wasn't aliens this time." Alma patted Jemma on the back. "If you take that job, we'll help solve all the cases."

"The job is in communications, not investigations," Jemma

said, using the words Tucker so often said to her. She helped clean up after the meal and put on a Warren Miller ski movie in the lounge for guests. Alma and Randy played hosts so Jemma retreated to her cabin and petted the kitties while she called the homeowners of the house Darryl Johnson sold for them. They had not authorized him to remove any furniture. Jemma e-mailed them photos of the Johnsons in the act of stealing but asked the owners to keep her name out of it. It wouldn't do for Jemma to be caught stirring up trouble while almost working for the sheriff.

DT lay in ambush for JK then jumped her, trapping her in a corner. Both bounded away when the phone rang. Jemma hesitated answering since the caller ID was blocked, but said a tentative "hello" anyway.

"Jemma, I hope I'm not interrupting anything."

"Karen, I was afraid it was a telemarketer calling. Is there a problem with your kitchen?"

"No. I was wondering if you saw something at Petula's that involved me?"

Jemma mentally searched the guest house. "Like what?"

"Something with my name on it. A file maybe. The detectives came by here today. They think I had something to do with her death. I swear, I didn't want to be president that bad. You have to believe me."

"Calm down, Karen. Don't get yourself worked up over this." What had Tucker said to her? "I haven't talked to him today, but I'm sure he was simply following procedure. He had to talk with everyone who might know anything."

"Are you sure? You know me, I don't have any secrets."

Know her? They'd first met only weeks before. "They're simply working their way down a list. Get a good night's sleep and forget about it."

"You're right. I'm boiling water over nothing. I'll take your advice."

After Karen hung up, Jemma wondered what she'd missed at the guest house that was so important.

Chapter 13
FRIDAY

$\mathcal{F}$RIDAY MORNING JEMMA renewed her vow to stay out of the investigation and to finish the corner cabinets that night before she quit for the day. Tucker said that he would be working long hours until this case was solved but planned to attend the party at Perfect for Framing that evening. Karen would be thrilled if Jemma could install the cabinets on Saturday. Working late last night had left only drilling holes for the hardware and putting on coats of polyurethane to be done. Between coats, she worked on bird houses and picture frames for the photos she sold at the family dude ranch.

Lottie had hung her bird house on her front porch so she could look at it out the living-room window. Jemma had to bend at the knees to get low enough to accept her hug. Come spring, Lottie said she'd find a better place for it.

As she worked, Jemma's mind was free to focus on the crime despite her best efforts to avoid the subject. Ward had to have done it. Petula had probably been a problem for years and the PI report had sharpened his fears in full color. At least he had taken his jealousy out on the right one and not on the man involved. Not that

Darryl was entirely innocent, but they met at her guest house, on her mountain and probably on her time schedule. He was a thief and an adulterer. Maybe he could have scaled up his taste for crime to murder. If Ward didn't cause Petula's death, then Darryl did.

It was after five when Jemma left, plenty of time to drive home, shower and dress for Ann Dixon's party at eight. She waved to Lottie in the kitchen and saw Travis standing behind her. Jemma left the workshop and had gone a couple of miles when the truck backfired. She slowed in surprise. The truck had been reliable up until now. She turned off the radio, then downshifted. Everything seemed smooth, then bang! It backfired twice, then bucked. Jemma pulled off the road and turned off the ignition.

Now what? The late afternoon winter light dimmed as she looked for a house to go to for a phone. She zipped up her jacket and grabbed her gloves and ski cap before getting out of the cab. A car swerved around her, the driver ignored her wave for help. No other vehicles came by. She stepped back into the cab, started the truck and drove but it backfired again. She wrote a note and stuck it on the driver's side window. The only defensive weapon she had was a long screw driver which she tucked up her jacket sleeve. Not that she would need it.

She pocketed the keys and stepped out of the cab in the last light of the early December evening. A truck pulled up behind hers onto the gravel. Her heart thudded; she was more vulnerable than she liked.

"Hey, Jemma." The lanky young man walked up to her.

"Travis. Perfect timing." She relaxed the grip on the screw driver. At least he was someone she knew. Trusting him was another matter. "I need a mechanic. My truck's not right."

"Tell me about it."

He stood a little too close to her, her back against the cab door. "It backfired, then bucked."

"Bucked, huh?" He stared at her lips.

Jemma tried to slide to the side when he blocked her escape. "What's going on?" She pushed against him but even with her height and strength, he didn't budge.

"I'm gonna let you start it again while I take a look and listen." He stepped aside, let her unlock and open the door. He grabbed her hand and helped her into the cab. When he reached for the hood latch, his arm pressed against her thigh, sending a slight shiver of fear through her. He pulled a flashlight from his pocket before walking to the hood and shone it on the engine while telling her to fire it up.

The truck started. Jemma put it in neutral, set the hand brake and got out. She didn't see anything amiss, like a broken fan belt or steam from the radiator.

Travis worked the throttle cable back and forth. It ran smoothly for seconds then sputtered to a stop. "You wait right here." Travis squeezed her with a quick arm around her waist.

Jemma tensed then removed his hand from her. "Travis Miller. You're over ten years younger than me. What are you thinking?"

He stepped back. "I like older women."

She watched him go to his truck and bring back a plastic bottle. He poured the contents into her gas tank.

"This here will fix you right up. Dry gas. You got water in your tank, maybe the last time you filled up." He closed the tank and gave her the empty bottle. "Soon as you can, get yourself a couple of bottles of this. Put in two when you fill up. Gas line antifreeze is good to have on hand in the winter 'cause of condensation." He closed the hood, looped his arm around her and led her to the cab door. "You didn't thank me for rescuing you."

Jemma opened the door, scrambled in and shut the door. She rolled down the window before starting the engine. It ran rough. "It's not fixed."

He rested his hands on the window frame. "It'll be rough till you get to a station at New Market. Bring it in Monday and I'll give it a thorough going over. I'll get you on the schedule."

"Thanks, I will." Jemma touched his hand with her gloved one.

He covered it with his free hand and held it a few seconds. "Sometimes younger is better."

Detectives Tucker and Graves parked beside the clean-up crew trucks, then met Ward as he walked from the guest house to the main house.

"Hello, Detectives. Come on in the house, it'll be quieter there." They went in and sat in the living room. "Would you like a drink?" When they declined, he poured himself a Scotch, added ice, and took a swallow. "It's been a difficult day. Do you have any news?"

"We're following leads, but nothing yet to build a case on." Tucker nodded toward the guest house. "You don't waste any time."

"I believe in getting things done. Procrastination's in the same category as embezzlement and forgery. All are a form of robbery."

Tucker looked around the room. "You've made some changes in here."

"A few. I took down my wife's photos. It was too hard to look at them." He jiggled the ice in his glass before taking another drink.

"Can you think of anyone who might want to harm your wife?"

"Besides some of the property owners up here? Most would want to harm me, like Darryl Johnson." He stared at the ice for a moment. "I kept telling Petula to let her brother Raymond make his own way, that he'd never pay her back for all the money she'd loaned him. He's one of those that spends money as soon as he gets it."

"Is there anything in her will?"

"She left most of it to me, of course. Ray gets only fifty thousand."

Graves wrote that down. "That's a lot of money to some folks."

"I suppose it is. But she doled out that much to him every year, so in the long run, he'd get less."

"Who else might want to harm you or her? Maybe someone wanted to get to you through her."

"The obvious would be Darryl Johnson because of his relationship with my wife. What you don't know is that I've blocked his request for an extension on a building loan. He's speculating on a development and has already overspent on the roads."

"That seems personal."

"You could be right, but I denied the extension before I received the report."

"How was your relationship with your wife?"

"Am I a suspect?"

"You tell us."

"I shouldn't be, even though I was here at the time. Petula and I had our problems but we cared for each other." The doorbell rang and Ward started toward the door.

"One more question. Do you plan to attend the POA meeting tomorrow?"

"Yes. I have some changes of my own I want to bring up."

The clean-up crew needed his attention so Detectives Tucker and Graves left. Once back at the sheriff's complex, Tucker studied the medical examiner's report about the death of Ann Dixon's husband last year. It was labeled "undetermined."

"It could have been nicotine tea," said Graves. "Or castor beans or rhubarb leaves."

"Convulsions weren't reported."

"Rhododendron?"

"No vomiting," Tucker countered.

"I know, yew leaves. They cause sudden death without warning."

"Are you studying poisons?"

"My wife's been reading mysteries lately."

"Go home. Eat. Get some sleep and clear your brain. Forget about poison." Tucker finished his log book and headed home to dress for the party. Tucker was only ten minutes late when he found a parking space in downtown Boone. A few snowflakes flittered down when he saw Jemma in a long coat and heels standing outside the gallery. "You could have met me inside," he said, wrapping an arm around her and opening the door.

"And miss my entrance with you?"

Tucker snuck a kiss to her neck under the guise of removing her coat. Her dress was red with sleeves past her elbows and a hem that stopped at her knees. She wore no jewelry but her hair was loose. He'd never seen it so shiny and wavy draped down her back to her waist. "We may have to cut this short."

"Oh?"

"I can't keep my eyes off of you. That's no way for a detective to act in public."

Her demure smile as she took his arm and led him to the finger food table registered in his chest. How could he be so lucky to have met up with her?

She handed him a plate and put some shrimp on hers. "I'm starved. I ran late and didn't have time to snack. I had trouble with the truck this evening, and, luckily, Travis came along and helped. He told me to make an appointment to have it checked over. I think he made a pass at me."

"You don't know?" He followed behind her and filled his plate.

"He's much younger than me. He's just a kid."

Her scoffing voice held indignation. Tucker chuckled. "Some say that about us."

"You don't see me as a kid, do you?"

A vision of a teenage Jemma tried to form in his head but she still looked the same – tall, long dark hair, easy smile.

"Don't answer that. Can we change the subject? I found out some interesting information to help you with your case."

"Why am I not surprised?" He led her to one of a dozen small tall tables placed around the gallery for people to eat while standing.

"Petula and her brother had an affair."

Tucker put down the shrimp he had speared with a fork. "Do you mean a party?"

Jemma leaned into his ear and whispered, "I mean as in sex in the guest-house bedroom. More than once."

Her warm breath sent shivers down his spine. "You're kidding. Look, this case is too important for you to tease me like that." Complications lead to possibilities.

"It's no joke. I have it from a reliable source."

Tucker glanced around, seeing the Boone mayor come in the door. "Who told you that?" He ate the shrimp, striving to look casual.

"I promised not to tell. Just like I promised you not to talk about the case to anyone else." Jemma's smug smile almost made him choke.

She had him there. "A reliable source?"

"I think so. But, it could be a frame to put the blame on the brother."

"What if I guess the source?"

"Nope. I gave my word. Did I tell you how handsome you look in your suit?"

He let her change the subject. He'd find out some other way. "Talk like that and I'll dress up for you any day." Tucker noticed several council members, the sheriff, bankers, real estate brokers, authors, artists, newspaper editors, the ASU chancellor and his wife. Darryl and Flora nodded as they walked by.

"Who are they?" Jemma asked, wiping her fingers on a napkin.

"Petula's boss at Star Lite Properties. What would you like to drink?" Tucker asked when a waiter carrying a loaded tray approached.

"Champagne."

Tucker lifted two flutes from the tray and handed one to Jemma.

Jemma's eyes lit up. "Here's to us solving the case."

Tucker countered with, "Here's to us." He sipped the drink. "Remember the kid who claimed his house was broken into by someone in a Pink Floyd t-shirt?" At her nod, he went on. "It was a hoax. The guy had broken his own front door by accident and made up the story so he wouldn't have to buy a new door."

"I hope they make him pay for all the police overtime."

"That's up to the courts."

The background music stopped and everyone gathered

around the base of the stairs. Jemma and Tucker stayed on the fringes of the crowd.

Louder music started and Elvis appeared at the top of the stairs singing, "One for the money, two for the show." By the time he reached "Don't you step on my blue suede shoes," everyone was clapping. Elvis sang his way down the stairs and to the front of the gallery. He removed the scarf from around his neck and handed it to Jemma without missing a note in "Danny Boy." Elvis' twenty minutes of music and gyrations ended with three encores and a crowd of happy people. Tucker caught himself singing along a time or two.

"Hello Jemma. Detective," Ann Dixon said. "Did you enjoy Elvis?"

"He was a great surprise. Do you know he lives near the ranch?" Jemma waved the trophy scarf. "Clinton has dinner with us on occasion."

Ann nodded. "Jemma, Flora wants to talk to you about photography." She led Jemma away but returned to Tucker. "Any progress on finding who killed Petula?"

"Progress? Yes. Do you have anything to add?"

"No. But I know Darryl and Flora didn't have anything to do with it. They wouldn't harm anyone."

"Unlike you. Something about Petula having a flat tire?"

Ann laughed. "I heard the tire took a couple of miles to go flat. Come on, Detective, you don't think I'd stoop so low as to give someone a flat tire, do you?" Ann finished her glass and snagged another from a waiter before excusing herself.

Clinton Triplett joined Tucker after changing out of his Elvis costume.

"Great show." Tucker said. "Jemma loved the scarf."

"Thank you, thank you very much," Clinton said in his Elvis voice.

"How well do you know Ann?"

"Been knowing her for years. I remember her and her brother before she stabbed him. He tried to cheat her out of

134

her inheritance when their parents died in a crash. He had a mean streak in those days."

"And now?"

"He works regular. Lives over in Tennessee with his wife and two daughters."

Clinton stopped Ann when she walked near. "May I use the phone?"

"It's over by the desk. If you want to block the caller ID, simply hit *67 before you punch in the numbers."

"Why would I do that?"

"I always do for personal calls in case I get a wrong number."

Jemma returned and tugged on Tucker's arm. "I want to show you something."

As they walked to a corner in the store, Jemma told him about Flora's request. "She wants to hire me to photograph her Elvis collection of memorabilia for insurance purposes. I scheduled it for tomorrow afternoon. I should finish with installing Karen's cabinets by noon."

"Good for you."

"I don't know if I want to. This is what I want you to see."

Tucker looked at the settee and two chairs for sale. "What am I looking at?"

"Remember when I followed the Johnsons and saw them taking stuff from a house?"

"Is this it? Are you sure?"

"Uh, huh." Jemma hesitated then looked at Tucker. "I contacted the owners and emailed them photos. They confirmed."

"You what?" Tucker's voice constricted down to a squeak.

Chapter 14
SATURDAY

SATURDAY MORNING JEMMA and Bo loaded the corner cabinets into the truck and made the trip around the mountain to Karen's house, careful of the black ice, frozen fog, on the road. Bo held up the cabinet while Jemma leveled and screwed it into the wall. By noon, the project was finished, the floor swept and Karen served them hot soup and sandwiches in her kitchen. Jemma had loaded the last of her tools and sat in the cab when an ambulance headed up the mountain. With a nod from Bo in the passenger seat, she followed the siren. She parked in her usual place at the Windsors' house, then was boxed in by two sheriff vehicles and a medical examiner's car.

She went to a woman standing in the yard and asked what happened.

"I phoned but Ward didn't answer. I brought him some lunch since he was all alone now. The door was open so I went in. He'd shot himself."

"How do you know?"

"He left a note. Something about the police hounding him. He wasn't up to living without Petula." The woman stopped when Detective Tucker approached them.

"Hello, ma'am. Did you find the body?"

"Yes. I guess we'll have to cancel the meeting this time." She turned to Jemma. "Who are you?"

"You need to tell him the whole story." Jemma turned and would have left but the only way down was on foot. She joined Bo in the cab. "I'm in trouble now."

"What's happened now?"

"I made Ward kill himself." Never again, she swore to herself. She would let Tucker do his job without her speculations.

"What?" Bo grabbed the cab handhold to straighten up and look at her.

Jemma gulped in air and wrapped her arms around her middle. "If I hadn't pushed Tucker to believe my theory that he killed his wife, none of this would have happened." Jemma covered her mouth and pleaded with herself that it was not so.

"Calm down. You're over-reacting. I can't see Tucker being pushed about anything. He's his own man. Not to take from you, but he just humors you."

"Huh." Why don't guys know that a woman hates to be told to calm down, she thought before registering Bo's words. "He humors me? Like one of his nieces?"

"I didn't mean it like that. It's just that a man's going to do whatever he's on the trail of and not be waylaid by emotions. He works on facts. You'd have to build a case to turn him to your way of thinking."

Jemma fell silent as she absorbed what he said. Tucker meant a lot to her but she couldn't be so sure that he felt as strongly about her. She took everything he said to heart and tried to do as he wanted, but that wasn't necessarily true about him.

Later after the body was put in the ambulance, the Medical Examiner drove away and all but one of the other vehicles was gone, Tucker approached the truck. "Ambulance chaser?"

"We finished at Karen's and the truck turned up the hill instead of down." Weak, even to Jemma's ears.

"What did the neighbor tell you?"

"Enough to know that if I hadn't made you go back and question Ward one more time, this wouldn't have happened," she blurted.

"I see. My training and experience aren't relevant."

"That's not it." Jemma's protest died with his next words.

"Bo, would you mind driving? I'm not sure she's in her right mind now."

TUCKER WATCHED THE TRUCK disappear down the crest of the hill before joining Graves in the study. "How does she do it? She gets to the crime scene before we do. You don't really believe she has anything to do with these deaths."

"No, I don't."

"I swear I haven't told her anything."

"She's just lucky. I was on the force only a few months when I proposed to my wife. I told her about some of the cases. She could see things that I missed, especially when a crime involved a woman. As long as it's between the two of you, who's to know?" Graves pointed to the suicide note, now enclosed in plastic. "This looks like his handwriting. It's the same as the writing on his desk calendar."

Tucker read the note, hand written on a lined tablet. "I don't want to go on without my Pet. She was a ray of sunshine in my otherwise dull life. The police are hounding me about killing her. I don't care about anything anymore. Ward."

Tucker re-read the text. "Weird note, don't you think?"

"I thought a banker would have more to say and say it better. He must have been out of his mind."

"That's true about all suicides in my book."

"Thirty-eight special. We may have found the missing gun."

"Forensics said it was wiped clean except for one set of prints. Remind you of anything?"

"The fireplace lighter."

"This whole scene has been set up. Ward was planning to attend the POA meeting today – look at the notes he'd added to his wife's file." Tucker passed the folder to Graves

"I see what you mean."

"He was perfect for framing for both his wife's death and his own."

"The investigation continues," Graves said as he led the way to the car and drove down the hill a short ways to Karen's house.

"Come in, detectives. Let me show you my kitchen." Karen clapped her hands like a kid playing patty-cake.

Tucker rubbed his hands over the drawer faces and tested the glides. Smooth.

"I have fresh coffee. Let me pour you some."

Tucker and Graves declined the coffee.

"Oh, you asked me about a file. This was in my mail box today."

She handed Tucker a large manilla envelope without stamps or post office inking. Tucker pulled out a pair of gloves from his pocket and put them on before handling the envelope. He took out the file folder with a label consistent with Petula's other files.

"I planned to call you but with everything that happened, I thought it could wait. Lucky for me, you stopped by."

Tucker opened the file and saw the same information that was on the computer. "Did you remove anything?"

"No, no." Karen stepped back and shook her head. "That's it. Nothing else." Her hand flitted to her throat.

Tucker looked at her. "Now's the time to talk, Karen. I found two of your gum wrappers behind Petula's house the day of the fire, the day this file went missing."

"I was never near her house, I swear. But there was something else in the file." Karen left and returned with a large photograph. "I don't know how she made this but it's a fake. I've never been alone with Darryl, much less in that position."

The photo was of two people in an embrace. The woman's face was Karen's; the man was Darryl.

"I don't own any clothes like that. I think someone wants to frame me. But Petula's dead."

"We'll take this. Thank you for coming forward. We have some more questions."

"Back to the living room, then." She hit the remote to turn on the gas fire.

"You have a good view of the mountains from the living room," Graves said. "Easy to see the goings and coming of your neighbors."

"I can see above the curve from the kitchen," she said.

"What did you see this morning?"

"Jemma brought the cabinets so I didn't see anything."

Although he suspected the answer, Tucker asked it anyway. "Do you like to hike?"

"Hike? Honey, do I look like I do? My idea of exercise is to go to Charlotte and hit the malls. Now that's my kind of fitness."

"Tell us some more about the proxies."

"It doesn't matter now. I will be president by default. I can't see anyone else coming forward."

"What about the vice president?"

"I hadn't thought of that." Karen stopped chewing her gum. "He could mess up everything."

"Oh?"

"The VP was tight with Petula, as far as meddling with our lives is concerned. At least he wouldn't flirt with the husbands." Karen smiled at her own joke.

Graves smiled but Tucker couldn't. Two people had been murdered. "It would take only ten minutes for you to walk up through the woods to get to the Windsor house."

"I suppose so, but why? Oh, you still think I'm a part of this? How could you? I couldn't hurt a mosquito sucking my blood." She glanced at the kitchen. "Besides, I was here all morning with the cabinet maker. Ask her. I was so nosy about everything she did with the cabinets."

"Thank you, ma'am. We appreciate your cooperation."

"We need to move fast." Tucker phoned the Ford dealership and found out that the rotating schedule had Travis off this Saturday. The drive to the Miller place was as quick as the windy roads allowed. "Mrs. Miller, I'm Detective Tucker and this is Graves. Is your great-grandson here?" She reminded him of his own grandmother, probably pragmatic and protective of family.

"Come on in, detectives. He's gone to the store and will be back any minute now. Have a sit in the kitchen."

They followed her into the kitchen where she was in the process of baking cookies.

"If you sit over there," she pointed to the far side of the table, "I can keep a lookout on the oven." She poured them coffee without asking and pointed to the sugar on the table. "Milk?"

The men shook their heads and she sat.

"You here on account of Petula Windsor's murder. My Travis didn't have anything to do with that. I know my boy. He's hard working, honest, always helping people."

"It's good that you think highly of him," Graves said.

"We want to clarify some points. What time did he leave this morning?"

"*This* morning? Early. He had lots of errands. You got lots of suspects? I bet it was her husband. He got tired of putting up with her bossiness."

"Oh?"

"Maybe he was in cahoots with the POA board members. They's tired of her pushing everyone around."

"You do say?"

"Not gonna tell me anything, are you? Maybe you suspect me."

The outer door opened and footsteps approached the kitchen.

"Did you kill Mrs. Windsor?" Tucker asked Mrs. Miller.

Before she could answer, Travis Miller came in and dropped bags of groceries on the counter. "You leave my Mamaw alone. She's innocent. She couldn't have done it."

"Oh?"

"'Cause I did it. I killed her."

Mrs. Miller jumped up. "Travis, there's no need –"

"Mamaw, I'm sorry. Don't say another word. I'll go with these detectives. Why don't you call your sister to come over so you won't be alone?"

"Travis, what are you talking about?" Mrs. Miller's voice squeaked. "You didn't kill that woman."

Tucker asked, "Did you change shirts or wash your hands this morning?"

"Huh? No. What are you talking about?"

Graves left.

"We'd like to take that shirt. Mrs. Miller, would you bring him another one?"

Travis jerked it off over his head and handed it to Tucker. "I don't want her to be alone."

Graves returned with a gunshot residue kit. Tucker put the shirt in the bag for the SBI lab, knowing the chance of finding residue after four hours was slim but the Chief had said to go by the book.

When Mrs. Miller returned, her great grandson put on the clean shirt. "Mamaw, call your sister."

Graves stayed behind while Tucker led Travis to the car and reminded him of his right to an attorney. When he refused, Tucker said, "Want to tell me about it?" then helped him in the back seat of the car and closed the door. Tucker went around to the driver's seat, got in and turned around to look him in the eye.

Travis didn't look at him. "Tuesday lunch I drove up the hill behind the workshop then hiked on up. I set fire to her house. She caught me, then tried to stop me."

"Why'd you do it?"

"I kept thinking about them taking Miller land from us and wanting more. They wanted us to chop down the trees and ruin my favorite hunting spot. Then, she lied about me years ago. See, she accused me of arson but it weren't true. She caught her own place on fire and picked me to blame it on. Setting fire to her place was fitting justice."

A car drove up and a man and woman went inside.

"That's Mamaw's sister. We can go now."

Once at the county law enforcement center, Travis was booked in. Tucker checked the files for an arrest history but since he'd been under sixteen, his juvenile record had been sealed.

They went over his statement. "How did you know Petula would be at the guest house?"

"I planned to have the fire started before she got there. She came early."

"Why did you know her schedule?"

"I, uh, you was right about me spying on her. I used to watch her regular, once or twice a week."

"Exactly what happened the last time you spied on her? In detail." Tucker knew he'd found the source of Jemma's story.

Travis' eyes glazed over and he stared at the wall. "I got closer, up on the porch. Petula got up from the bed, paraded naked to the vanity mirror, and pulled her hair down so's it fell over one eye." He relayed what he'd seen and ended with. "Then she kissed him."

"How do you remember it so well?"

Travis blushed. "I replay it in my head all the time." His eyes opened wide. "That's why I killed her. You see, Mamaw couldn't have done it."

After Travis was processed, Tucker and Graves returned to their car. "Fine little confession we got back there," Graves said. "He done tole on hisself."

"Soon as he thought we had his Mamaw, he was determined to protect her. Problem is, he was too quick."

"Why'd you bring him in?"

"He could be telling the truth. Everything fits. Plus, I thought we'd give him what he wants. He wants to be the hero. Let's go see how busy it is at Perfect for Framing."

The temperature was dropping and it was close to four when Tucker and Graves entered the busy shop. Christmas instrumentals played in the background. "Ann, we need to talk."

"Now?" Ann rang up a credit card purchase and handed the lady the slip to sign.

"Now."

Ann handed the lady her package and came out from behind the counter. "Just a minute." She said something to a woman who took over at the counter. Ann motioned for the detectives to follow her to her office. "Can you make this quick? It's a fabulous day and we're busy."

"Didn't you plan to be at the POA meeting this afternoon?"

"That's true, but it was cancelled. We're busier than I anticipated." Ann straightened her blazer as she sashayed behind her desk.

"Do you know why it was cancelled?"

"Poor Ward. I didn't know him well, but suicide is sad no matter who it is." Her words contradicted the satisfied look on her face.

"Your friend Karen will become president."

Ann nodded. "We'll vote by mail."

"You shouldn't have any trouble building your house now."

"I hope not. It's been a long and troubled, expensive time. I even had to spend six thousand to have the well fracked. Without that, the well gave less than a gallon a minute. Now it's up to three gallons a minute. I'm aiming to put all this needless hassle behind me." Her mountain accent crept in.

"These delays cost you quite a bit of money, with rent, lawyer fees, and the potential of losing your contractor," Graves said. "You're in a jovial mood."

"A tremendous dark cloud is gone from my life. The angst left and anticipation filled the void. You don't have anything on me." She nodded. "Don't you have anything better to do? If that's all ..."

"Mighty convenient, Ward's death. Mysterious, too. Like the way your husband died."

Ann collapsed in her chair. "What are you saying? That I'm somehow responsible for what happened to my husband? That's an out and out lie," she said, voice weakening.

Tucker let silence hover for a moment. "You stabbed your brother."

Ann's eyes widened. "He never pressed charges."

"Why don't you tell us about it?" Tucker gambled on the fifty-fifty chance she tell him.

"I had finished high school, he had finished a couple of years ahead of me, and we both still lived at home. He was a bully to everyone, including my parents but my dad could still control him when he needed to. When my parents both died in a car accident, they left everything to the two of us to split evenly.

"I knew right away that I'd have to leave. I couldn't stand against my brother alone. As soon as I heard they were dead, I packed my bags, loaded them in the car, and almost got out of the house before he came home. I figured I'd get my share through the court system after we sold the house."

Tucker nodded, encouraging her to continue. Her accent had reverted to those of her high school days.

"I went back in to get their wedding picture. I stopped in the kitchen to grab a soda when he walked in.

"'What are you stealing from me?' he demanded more than asked.

"I told him 'nothing.' You know everything gets split down the middle.'

"He said, 'We'll see about that. I already got myself a lawyer. The way I see it, I get it all.'

"I shouldn't have risen to his bait but I told him 'You never was right in the head, big man. Tough guys don't pick on those littler than them. What does that make you?' I didn't know better than to egg him on in those days.

"He started around the kitchen table. I threw the soda at him and grabbed a knife from the drain board. I managed to run out the front door when he grabbed me and swung me around. I kept hold of the knife and stabbed him below his collar bone. He let go and I ran to the car and got out of there."

"You had been pushed long enough," Tucker said, seeing the

situation through her eyes.

"I was scared but I have to tell you. It felt good when that knife went into him. He'd been mean to me all my life. He hasn't bothered me since. I'd do the same again."

"What happened with the house?" Graves asked.

"He lived in it for years. I sued him for half the value of the contents and he paid up. After ten years, he wanted to sell and move to Tennessee. By that time, the value had gone up. He had visions of keeping all the money but I faced him in the lawyer's office and he backed down. I haven't seen him since, but I do keep in touch with his wife."

Tucker stepped beside the desk, a little closer to Ann. "We have a few questions about Petula's death."

"I thought her husband killed her." She sat up.

"How would you know that?"

"The lady who found Ward told the board members, who then called to cancel the meeting."

"Exactly what did you hear?"

"That he was so jealous of her lover that he killed himself. He found that he couldn't live with himself and ended his own life. Isn't that right?" She looked from detective to detective.

"Parts of it. Ann, did you visit Petula on Tuesday morning?"

"I told you that. She refused to approve my house plans. I left them there."

"Did you see anyone else?"

"No one. I heard later that Ward was there but I didn't see him."

"Did she act nervous or different?"

She shook her head. "She was her usual hateful self."

"When your husband died, you made a formal complaint that Petula had caused his death." Tucker reviewed the report and the investigators found no foundation for her accusations.

"She did. He was too young to have a heart attack. I think she poisoned him with something that caused it. She planned on me selling out, but I fooled her."

Ann's grim smile chilled Tucker. "Did you have an autopsy done?"

"I paid for it myself but nothing conclusive showed up. It's still her fault. She made our lives miserable and all we wanted to do was build a house. She even complained about landscaping details to the inch."

"That puts you at the scene of the crime at the time of the crime and with a passionate reason." Tucker paused for his words to sink in. "Did you pretend to leave and sneak around back of her guest house and set fire to the place?"

"No, I did not."

"When she caught you, she ran back into the house to phone for help. You followed her and hit her over the head."

"No." Ann's voice cracked as she stood. "She was alive when I left."

"You didn't realize her husband was home. You planned to burn the house down and destroy the woman you hated in the process."

"No. I didn't know he was there – that part is true but not the rest of it."

"Did you kill Petula Windsor?"

"No. How many times do I have to tell you?"

"Why did you stab your own brother?"

Gasp. "He tried to cheat me."

"Same as Petula."

Chapter 15

*J*EMMA DROPPED OFF Bo at the ranch and stopped in to see if Alma needed her for anything. Alma finished up a phone conversation and Jemma glanced at the notes Alma had written. "Neck lift seven thousand dollars."

"What's wrong with your neck?"

Alma sputtered a denial then gave up. "I'm going to have my turkey neck fixed. It's my neck and I can do it if I want. The skier the other night got me to thinking about how I look. It's high time I fixed what I want to fix."

Jemma recognized defensiveness when she saw it. "Good for you. You do so much for everyone else. I'm sure Randy doesn't care but you're in the second half of your life and you have my permission to have whatever makes you happy." Jemma hugged her aunt.

Tears came to Alma's eyes. "Thank you. I couldn't take teasing right now."

Jemma hurried back to Boone for her appointment with Elvis. Flora took her to a room added onto the back of the house. She opened the door and light streamed in from a stained glass

Elvis window. An Elvis chandelier lit the room. Photographs, some signed, mirrors, clocks, album covers, ash trays, commemorative plates, Bourbon bottles, dolls – Jemma didn't know where to start. "Do you want overall photos of the room or shots of individual items?"

"Both, don't you think? The insurance company will need complete documentation. The original boxes are stacked in the closet. You don't need to photograph them individually."

"Let's get one of you next to the velvet portrait then I'll get to work." Jemma brought in supplemental lighting and worked for a couple of hours.

"Time for a break," Flora said. "I've made some coffee and have some peanut butter pie you have to try."

Jemma joined Flora in the living room.

After a few pleasantries, Flora brought up the fire. "Finding her like that must have been awful for you. You had to drag her down that long hallway, through the living room and over the threshold. You must be a strong woman."

"You know what they say, the adrenalin kicks in and you're stronger than a horse. When did you visit the guest house?"

"Me? I've never been there. I read about it in the paper. My imagination filled in the details. She may have looked good but she was trash. She's burning in hell now, to pay for her badness here." Flora dabbed her face with a napkin. "I was one of the first ones to befriend her when she first moved here. The bank put the house up for foreclosure sale and they bought it at auction."

"I heard about that." Jemma nibbled on the pie, reminding herself to ask for the recipe to give to Alma.

"I even forgave her for waiting until my husband's contract to sell it ran out. My husband and hers are Chamber of Commerce members. We socialized and I was good enough for her for about a year. I was thinner and cuter then." Flora tugged at the buttons on her blouse.

"What happened?"

"At one party, I overheard her telling a circle of women a

lie about me and my brother. She implied that he and I, well, hanky-panky, you get the picture. I confronted her and denied it but she just smiled that tight cold-eyed smile of hers. I swore I'd get back at her one day. Instead, I stopped attending those functions and turned to Elvis and cake." Flora ate a bite of pie. "And now Ward. I understand you were there right after his suicide."

Jemma took a moment to mentally fill in the grapevine points for Flora to have that knowledge so quickly. "You've talked with Ann."

Flora nodded. "We've been close friends for a long time. I'd do anything for her."

"And vice versa, I'm sure. You're fortunate to have a friend like that." Jemma put down her fork. "Wonderful pie. May I have the recipe for my aunt?" At Flora's nod, Jemma said, "I'll finish up for today in your Elvis room in an hour. It's so quiet back there I don't even hear traffic sounds."

"I know. I often sit in there and read." Flora picked up the plates and Jemma returned to work.

TUCKER AND GRAVES DROVE to the Johnson home. Jemma's truck was there. The road crews had sprayed liquid de-icer in lines down the town streets. Gone were the days of salting the roads and rusting the undersides of vehicles.

"My husband isn't here," Flora said, standing sleeveless and barefoot in the doorway.

"We'd like to talk to you, Flora."

"Me? What's this about?"

She didn't invite them in. "We need to ask you about your relationship with Petula Windsor." Tucker's breath puffed white in the air.

"I thought Ward's note explained all that."

"How do you know about Ward's death?"

"My friend, Ann Dixon, called when the POA meeting was cancelled."

"In that case, where were you this morning?"

"I went shopping for a New Year's Eve dress at South's in the mall and met a friend for lunch at the Broyhill Inn."

"What were you wearing?"

"Are you studying fashion, detective?" Her brassy sarcasm rang out.

Tucker frowned, trying to stay focused. Jemma must be inside taking Elvis pictures.

"My blouse is soaking in the laundry room. I spilled some sherbert on it at lunch. I hate that ammonia smell but if you want to see it ..."

Tucker nodded while Graves went to the car to retrieve an evidence collection kit.

"Have you washed your hands?" Graves asked while she led them to the laundry room.

"Many times. I thought Ward's death was suicide. You're acting like I'm a suspect."

"You have to admit that money was tight while you waited for the bank approval. You probably dropped five hundred dollars on a dress this morning. The timing is right." Tucker refrained from asking about Jemma.

"I charged it. It won't be due until January. Do I need a lawyer?"

"Are you guilty of anything?"

"Of course not."

Graves came in and collected the blouse and contents of the sink.

"Let's get this over with." Flora led them back to the front door.

Tucker hid his disappointment that he didn't catch a glimpse of Jemma. "Did you kill your rival, Petula Windsor?" Jealousy on top of blackmail would be a strong motive.

"No. I forgave my husband but I did make him promise to fire her."

Her easy response indicated she was prepared for the direct

question. Ann must have called and told about her own interview. "Did you kill Ward Windsor to protect your husband? He would have had access to his wife's records. He could continue the blackmail."

"What blackmail? I thought it was suicide."

"You need to come to the sheriff's complex to make a statement. We'll return the blouse once this is all over," Graves said.

"Keep it. I don't think I want to wear it again. You type up what I said and I'll sign it." Flora slammed the door behind them.

Jemma followed the noise. "Are you okay? I heard the door slam."

"It was nothing."

"I'm about done for today. I'll come back next week to finish up. Your collection is extensive."

"I know."

Jemma saw the distraction in Flora's face and quietly packed up her camera and equipment and left.

"Tell us about your morning, Darryl," Tucker said after barging into his office.

"I was right here. Saturdays are important sales days in the real estate business."

"I thought you dealt in commercial real estate."

Darryl remained seated. "That's mainly what we do. Even some commercial business is conducted on the weekend." His tone was wary.

"How was business?"

"Quiet. I answered the phone a few times. Christmas season is usually slow."

"Aren't you the owner? Why do you work on weekends?" Tucker leaned over the desk.

"This is a small office. My four agents and I rotate Saturdays."

"Did your wife call?"

He smirked. "She filled me in on your questions. Weren't

you rough on her?"

Tucker leaned in further, bracing himself on his hands. "Was I? Murder is rough – and final. Both for the victim and the guilty one. Are you guilty?"

Darryl rolled back his chair a few inches. "Of adultery? Yes. Of over-spending? Yes. Of living beyond my means? Yes. Of murder? No."

"You've lied to us before, claiming Petula was your only affair. What else did you forget to tell us?"

"What do you mean?"

Tucker dropped a sheet of paper on the desk. "Why did you sign an agreement to give Petula ten percent of your earnings? Most part time office help aren't paid in percentages."

Darryl snatched up the paper, glanced at it and tore it up.

"We have other copies."

"Of course you do. Petula's dead so this," he held up the torn pieces, "is null and void."

"It does provide motive. You sell over a million dollars of real estate a year. Giving her that much smells like a blackmail payoff. Any comment?"

Darryl shook his head.

"Can you prove you were here all morning?"

Darryl leaned in, his face closer to Tucker's. "Can you prove I wasn't?"

"Mind if we borrow your jacket?"

Darryl stalked to the coat tree, snatched the jacket and handed it to Tucker. "Not at all. By the way, that's mud on the sleeve, not blood." Darryl returned to behind his desk. "Next time you want to talk to my wife or me, do it in the presence of my lawyer. Otherwise, leave us alone. Do you understand?"

Tucker and Graves returned to the office, turned in the evidence and updated the chief by phone. It was then he found out that Travis Miller was out on bail. Lottie Miller's brother-in-law was a criminal lawyer from nearby Ashe County. Tucker called Raymond Vicarro's home, but only got the answering machine.

"Saturday night. He's out for a while. I'm heading home. Don't you have a date with Jemma tonight?" Graves shut down his computer and put on his winter coat.

"I'm heading her way in a few minutes. First I'm going to type up Ann Dixon's statement and stop by her house on the way to Triplett; her rental is just off Highway 105. See you Monday."

Soon, Tucker put the completed statement in his pocket, loaded a briefcase with notes to work on during the weekend and drove to Ann's house. A car he recognized was parked in her driveway.

Ann answered the door with a glass of champagne in her hand.

"May I come in?" Tucker asked as he slipped past her to the dining room. By the sideboard set with cheese and fruit stood Darryl and Flora Johnson. On the table was an opened Saslow jeweler's box.

"Would you care to join us?"

"What's the occasion?"

"Ann received an email from the vice president approving her house plans. As soon as the weather permits, she can begin building," Flora said.

"And I was just about to give my wife a long overdue gift." Darryl turned to his wife and raised a glass. "To a wonderful woman who has stuck by me through the good and the bad. I love you." The three clinked champagne glasses. He set down his glass, turned to Flora, then put the bracelet on her arm.

Flora twirled it around her wrist. "Thank you, dear. It's beautiful." She kissed him.

Darryl turned to the detectives. "Why are you here?"

"Following the jewelry. How did it get from Petula's guest house to here?"

"I took it from Petula's desk, from right under her nose." Ann raised her glass as if toasting herself.

"Let me tell you the way I see it. Flora was jealous of Petula and Ann wanted to make the POA problems disappear. One or both of you took care of her. Darryl wanted to get his loan extended and make his affair with Petula go away. Plus make the blackmail stop. The three of you worked together."

"Do you have any proof?"

"Not yet. However, that bracelet and box are evidence." The statement he'd typed remained in his pocket as he returned to his car. He heard Flora wail, "Do something, Darryl, he's got my bracelet."

A short time later, Tucker phoned Jemma from his car for their usual Saturday evening date. He avoided phoning while driving whenever possible, but he was running late. When she didn't answer immediately, he almost hung up to redial. "We've got to talk about this," he said after her "hello."

Tucker heard the floor boards squeak. Ward's death worked on her mind, he was sure. "Come on, Jemma. Everyone makes mistakes. We all call one wrong at some time. That's what learning is all about."

"There's got to be an easier way than someone killing themself."

"You sound terrible." Tucker turned onto old 421. "C-Girl, this isn't your fault."

"Yes it is. I made you go back and talk to him. Now we'll never know if he was guilty or not." Jemma sniffled. "Maybe I'm not cut out to be in law enforcement."

Tucker's inner "yee haw" hid beneath an enforced quiet.

"My instincts were way off. I thought he was glad to be rid of her."

"To begin with, you emphasized some points and I took them into consideration. I would have ignored you if they hadn't been worthwhile. I'm not trying to influence your career choice one way or another but quitting before you have the job would be like hanging up before you get the call." Tucker slowed when a car turned off in front of him. Even with his headlights, it was dark on the road, with few houses and no street lights. "I'm about to turn onto Elk Creek Road so we best hang up before I lose the signal. Be there in ten minutes."

Tucker slowed and turned right under the Blue Ridge Parkway. He downshifted as his headlights shone onto a light dusting of snow. His thoughts drifted to Jemma, blaming herself for something she didn't cause. He remembered feeling like that when he first joined the force.

Crunch!

Tucker grabbed the wheel with both hands. He checked the rearview mirror. He could just make out a vehicle with its lights off. As he heard its engine wind up, Tucker took his car out of low gear and sped up. He veered over the center line at the first bend but the vehicle bumped him again. He swerved in the dark. Again he was bumped. His car crossed the other lane. No guard rail.

He sailed over the bank and hit hard when the front wheels dropped to the ground. The steep dive stopped when he banged into something. A hot, powdery odor told Tucker the airbag had deployed. His face and arms burned. His left hand hurt when it hit the door from being flung from the steering wheel. He rubbed his right hand over his chest, glad he wore a ballistic vest or his chest would have burned also. A pounding began in his head when everything went black.

"He's twenty minutes late," Jemma said to Bo in the bunk house. "Something's happened." While Bo rounded up Wayne and Miguel, Jemma filled in Alma. Alma gave her a blanket and a thermos of hot coffee, in case the search took awhile.

"We'll take the top half of the mountain," Bo said to Wayne, who was driving the other vehicle.

Bo gave Jemma the spotlight and plugged it into the van's cigarette lighter receptacle. Halfway up the mountain, Bo slowed and Jemma methodically searched the edge of the road. She looked for scrapes on the guard rails, skid marks, anything out of the ordinary. "Go slower. So far all I've seen are fast food bags and beer cans." They reached the top, turned, repeated their trip down with Jemma in the back seat, light shining from the driver's side. Still nothing. Bo turned and went back uphill.

"Pull over at the upper end of this guard rail. I want to try on foot," Jemma said, panic closing her throat. Bo parked and they both got out, using hand flashlights.

"Wait. I saw something reflect. Over there." Jemma pointed with her flash light. "Oh, God, help me now."

"Let me go."

"No. I've got to get to him." Heart racing, panic in her throat, she took a step toward the edge.

"At least tie a rope around your middle. I'll attach it to the van bumper. Be careful." Bo honked the horn three long blasts to signal they'd found him.

Jemma slid over the side, one hand controlling her descent, the other holding the light. She could hear the ranch truck climbing up the road and come to a stop. Good. They'd alert the EMTs.

Careful not to touch the back of the car, she maneuvered to the driver's side before assessing the car's stability. It was wedged between two trees and wasn't going any further down the mountain. Tucker was strapped in, airbag deflated. She rapped the flashlight on the driver's side window.

No response. She tried to open the door but it was stuck. "Tucker," she yelled, slipped and held tight to the door handle.

A siren blasted the air above her.

"Tucker, talk to me." She pulled herself up and banged on the window again.

"Ma'am," a voice said beside her, "mind if we take over?"

Jemma felt herself set aside but refused to go back up the mountain. She stayed nearby but out of the way while they took Tucker out the passenger door. After his head was stabilized, he was put on a stretcher and hoisted up the bank. Jemma worked her way around the car and grabbed Tucker's briefcase and cell phone. Who knew how long it would be before the car was hoisted out of the trees?

Hours passed or was it minutes? Bo drove her to the hospital behind the ambulance. Tucker had come to but had only been allowed to say a few words to her. "My hero, C-Girl."

Bo drove her home around midnight. She couldn't sleep. To distract herself, Jemma turned on her laptop and looked at the photos she'd taken at the Windsor and Harmon houses, reviewing the before and after pictures of her carpentry skills. Time slipped by while she cropped, deleted and enhanced some of the photos before saving them in her portfolio file for construction. She zoomed in on one of Petula's desk. There was the threat letter, in front of the jewelry box. Petula couldn't admire the bracelet anymore, Jemma thought. She wouldn't be able to torment those trying to build in her neighborhood, she wouldn't be able to seduce the men in her life into following her whims. Wonder if she knew she had someone peeping in on her at times?

The check from Ward. Jemma hoped it cleared the bank before he killed himself. Don't they freeze accounts when someone dies? She'd probably find out about such technical things during her training for the sheriff's department. Ward's suicide. Would it ever leave her? It didn't seem right, not that she'd ever known anyone who committed suicide before. His actions didn't fit her limited image of someone about to take his own life. Weren't they supposed to be morose? Uninterested in anything? So sad they couldn't function? Or would they be hyper-organized to finish up, to give themselves closure? Wouldn't he have ensured that his wife's lover got punished?

If Ward took his own life, why didn't he wait until after the meeting? Petula had been so passionate about running the Property Owners Association.

Chapter 16

SUNDAY

*T*UCKER LAY IN the hospital bed, thankful that his only injuries were bruises and a possible concussion. The hospital was still running tests, watching for swelling around the neck vertebrae. His side hurt where his own gun jammed into him. "I had Graves bring in some photos and notes, in case you're interested."

"You did? Can't you get in trouble for that?"

"You can't let on to anybody about this. Swear?" She could be trusted, he'd realized sometime during the night.

"Yes, sir. Not even Brandy. I was so afraid you would never trust me again, after all that stuff I said ended up in the newspaper."

"This is your second chance, C-Girl. Something about this suicide doesn't make sense. Ward scheduled you to rebuild the porch and he had hand-written notes about things to do next week." He handed Jemma the photos.

She studied each one, not saying anything. She put everything down and looked at him. "Why were you run off the road? I mean, you aren't the only detective. Graves or someone else would have taken over the case. What could have triggered someone to do that?"

"I had just left the Johnsons and Ann Dixon. I spoiled their celebration which reminded me of that bit in *The Wizard of Oz* when the wicked witch was killed." Tucker shifted in bed to a more comfortable position.

"And then they were off to see the wizard. Only in this case, the witch and wizard were both dead and you had collected the evidence. Did they say anything incriminating?"

"No one admitted to murder, if that's what you mean."

"They could easily have followed you to get back at you for harassing them."

"No one else knew I was there or that I would be seeing you that night." Tucker wished he recognized the vehicle but it was too dark. If only the state would use front bumper license plates in addition to the rear ones ...

"We see each other every weekend. Travis would have heard about that. He could have parked off to the side at the top near the Parkway and waited. You wouldn't have noticed a car parked there because people use that area for car pooling."

"Maybe it was a warning."

"Maybe it was intended to make you victim number three. After two killings, what's one more?"

Tucker wouldn't dwell on what could have happened; it was wasted mental energy.

"What else do you have?"

"Copies of the suicide note, Petula's fire photos, break-in photos, PI report and photos."

"Let me see the PI stuff ... er, evidence."

Tucker'd been over everything a dozen times and couldn't pinpoint the problem. He asked Jemma to adjust the pillow so he could be more comfortable. Snowflakes gathered on the hospital window sill.

"If it wasn't suicide, how did someone get close enough to kill Ward? And what about the note? It was in his handwriting." Jemma stood. "You be Ward behind the desk and I'll be the killer." She walked to the hospital room door.

"He must have let the person in since Ward normally kept the front door locked. They both went to the study." Tucker pushed the button to raise the head of the hospital bed.

"The killer could have pulled the gun immediately or waited until they were in the room. I guess it doesn't make any difference. Either scenario would work." Jemma walked to the bed.

"Ward could have been forced to write the note, then he was killed with his own gun."

Jemma sat on the bed. "Let's review what we have." Jemma wrote down some names.

"Darryl and Flora Johnson should be listed separately."

"Flora could have killed Petula because of jealousy. Why would she kill Ward?"

"Good question. Put that down. Why would Darryl kill Petula? Put down blackmail. His problem was Ward blocking a loan. The damage was done as far as the affair was concerned."

Jemma wrote that down. "Maybe she did Petula and he did Ward. Their only alibis are each other."

"Someone could have seen their cars. Maybe you did. You said you passed a couple of cars on the way up the mountain."

Jemma looked at the PI photos again. "Where did the photographer park when he took these? The house above Karen's belongs to summer people. Anyone could have parked there then walked through the woods up to the Windsor house."

"Put down Ann Dixon. She desperately wanted to build that house as a memorial to her husband. She's been huffing and puffing about Petula's maneuvers. She stabbed her brother. Violence is in her makeup."

"Aren't women more inclined to poison?"

"Statistically. She was in the neighborhood the day of the fire." Tucker rubbed his shoulder, reluctant to admit to all over pain. Every bone and muscle in his body reacted to yesterday's jostling.

"If Petula set the fire to ignite the POA into paving the road, anyone could have come upon her. When she ran away into the house, anyone could have hit her with a rock, then dropped it along the road."

"Karen Harmon could have taken care of the Windsors." Tucker explained about the gum wrappers and file folder.

"Could Petula have framed her? I'd hate for it to be Karen. What about Petula's brother, Ray?"

"He inherited a little from his sister. What reason would he have to kill his brother-in-law?"

"Next is Travis Miller. Old wrongs fester in some people. Petula had recently wanted more land to cut down trees so she could have a better summer view. That would destroy Travis' hunting spot, not to mention shrink his inheritance. Kill them both off to complete the revenge. Plus, he doesn't mind using a truck to get what he wants." Besides, he'd set up Jemma with water in her gas tank.

"He saw something. I mean, he could have seen something." Jemma shook her head. "Where's that suicide note?" Jemma read the note, then smiled.

Tucker looked at the note. "What did you see?"

Jemma showed Tucker, who then gathered up the files. "I better call Graves and get a warrant."

After the phone call, Tucker rummaged in his briefcase and brought out a box casually wrapped in a plastic shopping bag. "I had planned to give you this for Christmas but I'd rather do it now. I've thought long and hard about this." He handed her the package.

Jemma fumbled, almost dropped it getting it out of the bag. "What?"

"It's a cell phone. I've been concerned about your safety, with the truck problem the other night. I know it's not romantic, but it shows that I'm concerned about you."

Jemma blinked, then smirked, then laughed.

Tucker pulled up the covers. "What's so funny?" Why was she acting like this? Was his practical gift so strange?

Jemma picked up the Saslow's jewelry case and flashed it at him, then picked up the cell- phone box.

"You thought?" Tucker smiled. "But you don't wear jewelry."

Jemma was tickled; she couldn't stop laughing and nodding her head.

How could he help himself? He joined in her laughter until his side ached.

"What was so funny?" he asked once they had quieted.

"I was afraid you were going to go serious on me."

"You mean as in legal?"

"Something like that. I'm relieved ... make that happy. I think we're doing fine the way we are. Not moving too fast."

"Come here, C-Girl. Lay on this bed with me, I don't care what the nurses think."

She snuggled in bed beside him in the crook of his shoulder. "I've a present for you, too."

"Oh?" He looked around the room but didn't see anything wrapped.

"I've decided not to accept the position at the sheriff's department."

His heart thumped in his chest, and not from the injuries. "What made you decide to do that?"

"Too confining. My riding and photography would be curtailed and my cabinet work's beginning to have a reputation. Do you mind?"

"That's the best present you could give me. One person in law enforcement in this duo is enough."

Jemma leaned over him and looked into his eyes. "I do expect you to let me help you with cases, unofficially."

"Now, Jemma. I can't promise you that. You're helping tomorrow, that should be enough for a while."

"For a while. Besides, I can always re-apply."

Chapter 17
MONDAY

"**T**HANK YOU FOR fitting me in so early this morning." Jemma handed the head mechanic the truck keys.

"Travis said it was an emergency. He wants to work on it himself." He keyed in the truck information to the computer and took the work order toward the shop.

Jemma went to the waiting area and called Tucker on her new cell phone, squinting to see the tiny display. He'd programed in his various numbers yesterday. This was her first call, and it thrilled her that it was to him.

"The search warrant only turned up copies of the PI report, linking him to the break-in." She could hear the frustration in his voice.

"What can I do?"

"Nothing. I'll go back through and search again."

"You get all the action."

"I'll tell you about it later, C-Girl."

"Wait. I have an idea. We'll let him find it. You get out of sight and hide the cars." She explained and went to the repair desk.

"May I speak with Travis for a minute?"

164

"Sure thing. I'll have him meet you over by the cashier office." He phoned for Travis.

Fresh rubber odor from the stack of new tires on display followed her to the cashier area. "Any problems making bail on Saturday?"

Travis shook his head. "We have a criminal lawyer in the family. What's this I hear about the detective being hurt?"

"He's doing fine. In fact, he's in the process of getting a warrant to check the homes and vehicles of a number of suspects."

"I lied to protect Mamaw. She explained it all to me. I didn't have anything to do with the murders or his accident. I swear."

Jemma glanced to make sure she had the attention of the office help. "I believe you."

"What's he looking for?"

"Front end damage to a vehicle and some sort of blunt instrument used to hit Petula Windsor over the head." Jemma moved away from the counter and whispered, "I know you weren't involved."

"Thank you. I, uh, apologize for pestering you last week. Sorry about the water in the gas tank trick. I want you to know that I've asked a girl out on a date."

"Good for you. Who is she?"

"We went together in high school but she moved away for a year or so. I found out she was back and called her. I'm meeting her after work."

The cashier was on the phone when Jemma left for the waiting area inside the sales area. She wandered over and made herself a cup of coffee, taking as much time as she could. She studied the posters and displays and was about to resort to looking at actual cars when Ray came out of his office and asked the cashier for keys and a tag.

Once he drove away, Jemma waited all of five minutes before dashing back to Travis, mindless of the mechanics telling her she wasn't allowed in the shop. "I need to borrow your truck. Now."

"Nobody drives my truck but me. I'd like to oblige but I can't do that."

"Drive me, then."

Travis stared at her, then grinned. "That was a setup, wasn't it? You think it's Ray. I'll drive you, Jemma. Let me tell the boss." He wiped his hands and dropped the shop towel on his tool chest. They drove through the wet streets and parked behind Ray's loaner car, blocking him in; then they got out of the truck and waited. "Something else I remembered about Ray and his sister that gave me the creeps. She told him that she'd always admired his body, even when he was a boy, ever since his father married her mother when they were kids. She said she'd always loved the fact that she had introduced him to the physical side of love when Ray was twelve and she was sixteen. Said she needed to practice so she could snag herself a man, as they would say around here."

Jemma's jaw dropped. "Why, that's her brother. Stepbrother, which still isn't right."

Ray ran from the back yard, followed by a sluggish Tucker. Jemma picked up a rock from the yard. Ray veered off the path to avoid the car and sped toward the woods.

"Hey Ray," Jemma yelled.

Ray glanced over his shoulder and then sidestepped the rock she'd thrown. It was enough of a delay.

Travis sprinted and tackled Ray. When he hit the ground, a rock and car keys tumbled from his hand.

Tucker hauled Ray up and handcuffed him. "Fast work, Travis."

Jemma winced at the thought of the pain Tucker had to feel. All those bruises and strained muscles. None of it showed in his face.

"Yes, sir." Travis stood and dusted off his work pants.

"That's mine. She gave me that," Ray said as Graves bagged the painted rock.

"When?"

"Thanksgiving. I made it for her when we were kids."

"Wrong answer. When we find Jemma's prints on it, it will prove it was in the house shortly before her murder. Probably trace blood also." Tucker knew it was a long shot.

Jemma came up to him and looked him in the eye. "I thought you loved her."

Ray crumbled. "I did! I did!" Tucker kept a hold on Ray's arm. "I'd do anything for her. She knew that."

"You have the right to remain silent, the right to an attorney – "

"It doesn't matter any more. She's gone. I didn't mean to kill her. I did the break-in like she wanted. I left the gum wrappers and left the envelope at the neighbors days later. She had to find out what was in that report. She made copies and had me slip one on her boss' desk."

Tucker brought both of Ray's hands to his back and slipped on handcuffs.

Jemma nodded, as Ray kept his gaze on her.

"She was so mad at the property owners, she wanted to make a point, make sure they voted to pave the road. It was her plan for me to bring shop towels and start the fire. I parked down below and walked up through the woods, like I always did. Only this time, I kept seeing those photos in my head. She shouldn't have cheated on me like that."

"Wasn't she married?" Jemma asked.

"He didn't count. He was just her ticket to success. Once she was gone, I got the idea of framing him from Pet. She set up the frame-up for the fire. I copied her. Ward was perfect. It almost worked. What gave me away?"

"Ward never called his wife 'Pet.' You were the only one who did."

"That's not much to go on."

"Ward used the word 'ray' in a sentence. Detective Tucker said the note didn't sit right with him. It could have been a private joke you used when you dictated the note or it could have been a clue left by Ward."

"Is that it? You set this trap based on one word in the note?"

"I took another look at the photos from the fire, the ones of the bedroom. Something was missing from the vanity." Jemma checked with Tucker before saying more. He didn't stop her.

"What wasn't there?"

"The pet rock that you made for your sister when you were kids. I thought you'd want to keep it. It was there when she gave me a tour of the place."

"I was afraid Detective Tucker was getting close. That's why I tried to scare him off," Ray said.

"Why did you turn her over?" Jemma had to know.

"I wanted to see her face one last time. I didn't mean to hit her. She died in my arms."

Graves brought the car from its parking place at a neighbor's house and loaded Ray in the back seat.

Jemma drove the loaner car and Travis returned to work on Jemma's truck.

CHRISTMAS MORNING, TUCKER JOINED the Chase friends and family at Blue Falls Ranch. She gave DT and JK some special treats. The family had long ago stopped giving elaborate gifts but instead favored tokens. Those ranch hands who either had no home to go to or couldn't afford the trip also gathered in the ranch game room. Jemma's parents, on their first day back from their cruise, had given the wranglers a cash bonus. Other small gifts were exchanged before Jemma went to a supply closet she'd filled the night before. Life was good for Jemma. Ann Dixon had called and wanted to carry more of Jemma's photos in her store. Flora still wanted her to photograph her Elvis collection even though her hearing for theft was coming up in a few days. Tucker had fully recuperated from the crash. And Jemma knew in her heart that Tucker wasn't interested in other women.

"I've built each of you," Jemma said after she'd called for everyone's attention, "a house."

Stunned silence greeted her.

"Not a house for you to live in." She retrieved a gift from the closet and held it up. "A bird house." Laughter encouraged her. "This one is for Tucker." The jailhouse design was complete with bars on the windows. The wranglers each had variations on the bunkhouse, and her parents had miniatures of the ranch lodge and the barn. Alma's looked like an old iron cookstove with the open oven door as a landing pad.

Bo reached over and took Wayne's birdhouse. "I like this one better."

"No way. She made this one for me."

Jemma looked at Tucker, then returned the birdhouses to the appropriate wrangler. "Boys, didn't you learn anything? Jealousy and possessiveness can get you killed."

THE END

Peel a Pound Soup

2 large cans tomatoes
2 lbs. Carrots,
  peeled and sliced
1 large onion, diced
2 cans beef broth
  or veggie broth
1 pkg. Lipton onion
  soup mix
1 bunch celery, diced

1 large head cabbage,
  chopped
2 cans green beans
2 green peppers,
  chopped
1 Tbsp. Salt
1 tsp. Pepper
1 tsp. Curry
1 tsp. Lemon pepper

In a large 8 quart kettle put tomatoes, onion, soup mix, celery, green beans, green peppers and carrots and cover with water. Boil on high heat for ten minutes. Then reduce to low and simmer until vegetables are tender. Add broth, salt, pepper, curry powder and lemon pepper. Simmer until broth is hot.

Pan Fried Trout

4 fillets
3/4 cup buttermilk
3/4 cup flour
1/4 cup cornmeal

½ cup olive oil
1/4 tsp. Salt
1/8 tsp. Pepper
Mustard-dill lemon sauce

In a large plate, soak trout in buttermilk. Drain briefly. On a sheet of waxed paper coat fillets with a mixture of flour, cornmeal, salt and pepper. Place oil in heavy cast iron skillet over medium high heat. Fry fish until golden brown on one side. Turn and brown other side. Serve with Mustard-dill lemon sauce.

Mustard-Dill Lemon Sauce

1/4 cup snipped
  fresh dill
2 Tbsp. Red onion,
  diced finely
2 Tbsp. Parsley, chopped

1 tsp lemon zest
1/4 cup oil
2 Tbsp Dijon mustard
2 Tbsp lemon juice
1 Tbsp honey

In a medium bowl combine; whisk until well blended and smooth.

Spicy Orange Beets

2 cans (16oz) beets
1/4 cup brown sugar
1 Tbsp grated orange rind
2/3 cup orange juice
2 tsp cornstarch

2 Tbsp butter
1/4 tsp salt
1 Tbsp chopped fresh chives
1/4 tsp allspice
1/8 tsp pepper

In saucepan combine sugar, orange rind, cornstarch, salt, allspice and pepper. Gradually add orange juice, stirring until smooth. Stir in butter and bring to a boil, stirring constantly. Boil 1 minute, stirring constantly. Add beets; cook until thoroughly heated. Sprinkle with chives before serving.

Scalloped Potatoes

5 medium potatoes,
  peeled, sliced, cooked,
  drained
Salt to taste
1 stick margarine

2 Tbsp cornstarch
1 cup milk
1 cup Cheddar cheese
Dash pepper

Mix cornstarch, milk, margarine, salt and pepper in a small saucepan. Cook over medium heat until sauce begins to thicken. Place potatoes in a baking dish and pour the sauce over them. Sprinkle cheese over the top. Put in a 350 degree oven only long enough to brown.

Better Than Sex Yellow Cake

1 yellow cake mix
1 box regular vanilla
  pudding mix (not instant)
1 can (15 oz) crushed
  pineapple

1 container (8 oz) whipped
  topping
1 cup sugar
1 can coconut

Bake cake by the directions on the package in a greased and floured 13 x 9 inch pan. Mix sugar and pineapple and bring to a boil. Boil 1 minute. Punch holes in hot cake and pour pineapple mixture over cake, evenly. Fix vanilla pudding according to directions on the package and then pour evenly over pineapple. Cool in refrigerator. When cool, top with whipped topping and then sprinkle with coconut.

$\mathcal{M}$AGGIE'S LOVE FOR CSI, the Appalachian Mountains, and outdoor activities collectively have influenced her mystery series. In the past Maggie vacationed on several dude ranches inspiring her to create one just outside of Boone where her character Jemma resides. The mountains are such an important part of her story that Maggie stated "they are almost a character in the book."

Residents of Boone will also find some familiar characters featured in her novels. Joe White, Pearle and Lyle Bishop, Bill Kaiser, Bob and Ginny Mann from the Todd General Store, and Clinton Triplett (Elvis) are locals, depicted as they are in real life.

Maggie settled in the Appalachian Mountains in 1993 with her husband and cat. She founded the High Country Writers organization in 1995 and is an avid lover of the outdoors. *Perfect for Framing* is her fourth novel set in the area. Maggie has gained broader popularity and has been featured in the Houston Chapter of Sisters in Crime publication as a recommended mystery author. She was selected in 2007 as one of "100 Incredible Women" from Eastern Carolina University.

Visit Author Maggie Bishop's websites at:
http://maggiebishop1.tripod.com
http://appalachianadventure.tripod.com
http://mmurderatbluefalls.tripod.com

Murder at Blue Falls
by Maggie Bishop

ISBN: 1932158758

Paperback: $12.00

Jemma believes she just wants peace – and thinks she'll find it leading trail rides and doing carpentry on her parents' dude ranch in the Triplett Valley. A series of minor crimes escalates to arson and murder, and Jemma's diversion as an amateur CSI puts her life in danger. Detective Tucker's suspicions disturb and annoy our heroine, but in the end he becomes the answer to her prayers.

"An established must-read romance author, Maggie Bishop has crossed into the mystery genre with finesse. Her latest novel is packed with suspense around a tightly-woven plot which begins with the poisoning of dogs and escalates to the murder of a local man. Throughout, she deliciously teases the reader with the bristly attraction between the investigating detective and the woman who found the dead man's body and who just might be a suspect. Set against the beautiful backdrop of Boone, North Carolina, with engaging characters, red herrings at every turn, and a galvanizing story line, this is a must-have, must-read. Highly recommended." -- Christy Tillery French, **Midwest Book Reviews**

Visit Author Maggie Bishop's websites at:
http://maggiebishop1.tripod.com
http://appalachianadventure.tripod.com
http://mmurderatbluefalls.tripod.com

Appalachian Paradise
by Maggie Bishop

ISBN: 0971304564 Paperback: $9.95

Athletic career woman meets good-ole-boy for a five day backpacking trek in the rugged North Carolina mountains. Appalachian born Wes triggers Suzanne's resentment and her desire amongst boars, bears and Girl Scouts. Suzanne's pack and old hurts lighten as Wes' easy charm helps her truly see the hope and allure of spring flowers, love and forgiveness.

Emeralds in the Snow
by Maggie Bishop

ISBN: 1932158561 paperback: $12.00

Emerald Graham and Lucky Tucker are an unlikely pair. She, accustomed to a life of privilege in which everything's a bit of a game, including her teaching career. He, who has not let his life of struggle keep him from giving to his family, his community and the skiers he rescues on Sugar Mountain. Yet they seem to be finding an uneasy bliss when a treasure hunt and an old murder mystery threaten all they value.

175

Welcome to books from
High Country Publishers of
INGALLS PUBLISHING GROUP, INC.

For more information on books and ordering and
links to authors' websites, visit our main website at:
www.ingallspublishinggroup.com
www.highcountrypublishers.com

Visit Author Maggie Bishop's websites at:
http://maggiebishop1.tripod.com
http://appalachianadventure.tripod.com
http://mmurderatbluefalls.tripod.com

High Country Publishers

INGALLS PUBLISHING GROUP, INC